THE CONVENIENT ENGAGEMENT

The De Petras Saga, Book 5

Emily E K Murdoch

DRAGONBLADE PUBLISHING, INC.

ARE YOU SIGNED UP FOR DRAGONBLADE'S BLOG?

You'll get the latest news and information on exclusive giveaways, exclusive excerpts, coming releases, sales, free books, cover reveals and more.

Check out our complete list of authors, too!

No spam, no junk. That's a promise!

Sign Up Here

www.dragonbladepublishing.com

Dearest Reader;

Thank you for your support of a small press. At Dragonblade Publishing, we strive to bring you the highest quality Historical Romance from some of the best authors in the business. Without your support, there is no 'us', so we sincerely hope you adore these stories and find some new favorite authors along the way.

Happy Reading!

CEO, Dragonblade Publishing

Additional Dragonblade books by Author Emily E K Murdoch

Twelve Days of Christmas
Twelve Drummers Drumming
Eleven Pipers Piping
Ten Lords a Leaping
Nine Ladies Dancing

The De Petras Saga
The Misplaced Husband (Book 1)
The Impoverished Dowry (Book 2)
The Contrary Debutante (Book 3)
The Determined Mistress (Book 4)
The Convenient Engagement (Book 5)

The Governess Bureau Series
A Governess of Great Talents (Book 1)
A Governess of Discretion (Book 2)
A Governess of Many Languages (Book 3)
A Governess of Prodigious Skill (Book 4)
A Governess of Unusual Experience (Book 5)
A Governess of Wise Years (Book 6)
A Governess of No Fear (Novella)

Never The Bride Series
Always the Bridesmaid (Book 1)
Always the Chaperone (Book 2)
Always the Courtesan (Book 3)
Always the Best Friend (Book 4)
Always the Wallflower (Book 5)
Always the Bluestocking (Book 6)
Always the Rival (Book 7)
Always the Matchmaker (Book 8)

Always the Widow (Book 9)
Always the Rebel (Book 10)
Always the Mistress (Book 11)
Always the Second Choice (Book 12)
Always the Mistletoe (Novella)
Always the Reverend (Novella)

The Lyon's Den Connected World
Always the Lyon Tamer

Pirates of Britannia Series
Always the High Seas

De Wolfe Pack: The Series
Whirlwind with a Wolfe

CHAPTER ONE

March 7, 1814

S APPHIRE GIGGLED AS she watched the argument unfold. There was nothing quite like a family for bringing out those well-meaning arguments, was there?

"I say it was October," Coral said firmly. "And I distinctly remember because—"

"It was November, and I will swear that in a court of law if I have to!" said Micah, a teasing air in his expression. "And the longer you go on about it, the more I am convinced you are entirely wrong!"

Sapphire tried not to snort with laughter at the look of out-rage on her eldest sister's face. Coral's marriage five years ago had certainly softened some of her sister's edges, but her absolute determination that she was correct about everything was probably not something that would ever disappear.

Micah was teasing. At least, Sapphire was almost sure he was teasing. Their brother had a certain way of getting under people's skin, particularly Coral's.

When had the siblings last seen eye to eye?

"Do not argue, it does not matter," interjected Emerald, concern in her eyes.

Sapphire watched them continue to bicker, despite the third

de Petras sibling's request for calm.

That was always the way with them. Their dinner every Thursday evening—perfectly chosen, apparently, to avoid clashing with any invitation from the *ton*—usually descended into some argument or other.

Politics, art, whether so-and-so would be engaged by the end of the Season, whether that person's ball was more impressive than someone else's…

There never was a family like the de Petrases for getting themselves tangled in knots.

"Mama, do something," Sapphire heard Emerald murmur. "You must—"

"Oh, there's no must about it, I am afraid," said Opal de Petras with a gentle smile. "You know your siblings."

Emerald sighed, and Sapphire wondered what it must be like to be Emerald. Always quiet, always shy.

"Regardless of when it happened, then," Robert tried to interject, glancing at his wife Emerald with concern, "continue your story."

It was well done, even Sapphire had to admit. He was, perhaps, her favorite brother-in-law. Not that one should have favorites, or that anything was wrong with Edward, Coral's husband.

But there was something far more intimidating, talking to a duke.

"Come, you know they have far more fun bickering than the rest of us would have enjoying a calm conversation," cut in Catherine, Micah's wife, with a laugh. "Sometimes I think the two of them would argue with the world if they could manage it!"

Gentle laughter meandered around the room as all those present agreed with her.

"Well, I'm the eldest," same Coral primly, mischief dancing in her eyes. "So you will just have to take my word for it."

Micah groaned. "Always with the eldest, you cannot always

hold that against me!"

"And to think," came a voice from the corner, "if Micah had been the heir, it would be Coral who would have to accept *she* was wrong!"

The laughter around the room came to an abrupt halt. Sapphire swallowed as her stomach churned.

All eyes turned to the latter speaker. Amethyst de Petras, their cousin; their cousin who had arrived most suddenly a few years ago, and just recently had been announced as a co-heir to the estate by her aunt. Their mother.

The trouble was, of course, that though she was family, she was not...well. *Family.* Sapphire could think of no other way to describe it. She was a cousin, and she was a de Petras, and she had lived with them ever since she had arrived in London, but...

Well. There were some things one could say to a sibling, and those were usually the things you would never permit anyone else to say. It appeared her cousin had just realized that.

Amethyst's cheeks flushed as she stammered, "I-I mean—all I meant was—"

"We know full well what you meant, thank you," said Micah curtly.

"Now come on, the story," said Sapphire hurriedly, rising to pick up the bowl of delectable chocolates which her father had brought home as a treat only that afternoon. "You were going to Bath, and you saw Prinny."

Coral caught her gaze and a flash of momentary understanding moved between them. "Yes—yes, I saw Prinny. My, what a strange shock I had, to discover..."

Sapphire offered the bowl of chocolates wordlessly to Micah, whose hackles still appeared to be raised, but he said nothing as Coral continued her story.

It was strange, Sapphire mused as she slowly traversed the whole room, offering the sweet refreshments to all—ensuring Amethyst took two.

It was difficult to join a family. Truly join one, to become a part of the landscape, an expected member of every gathering. To join in with the jokes that took a lifetime to grow, to understand the quips and references to events that occurred before one's lifetime.

How did one simply fit into a family?

It was rather like marriage, she supposed, as Sapphire sat, the bowl of chocolates laid carefully beside her, right where she could snaffle a few while the others were not looking.

After all, all her siblings had now wed, joining families very different from their own, and had undoubtedly been forced to learn different ways of teasing, of jesting, of laughing. She supposed the only difference was that Amethyst had no spouse to help ease her into it.

"—and he said, of course not, that's not my job!" Coral finished triumphantly.

Sapphire started as the room erupted with laughter, gentle applause from Jasper, her father, at the telling of the tale.

Bother. She had entirely missed the middle, and the ending simply did not make sense without it.

"Well said, Coral," said Edward firmly.

"Yes, hear, hear," Catherine said with a smile, her hand resting gently on her husband's as they sat beside each other on the sofa. The swelling of her stomach was obvious now, her other hand resting upon it.

Sapphire watched with interest as Micah's jaw tensed before he spoke.

"Very good."

It was a marvel, thought Sapphire with fascination. The way her brother had mellowed since he married Catherine. The family should be thanking her on bended knee, really, after the mischief he'd got up to.

"And how is Beryl?" Catherine asked Emerald, clearly eager for the conversation to shift in an entirely different direction.

Emerald, though usually monstrously shy, beamed as she started to speak of her eldest child. "Oh, coming along well, I must say. The new governess…"

Sapphire stopped paying attention. Well, she saw Beryl almost every day, there was little news she could be given on that score. Her nieces were the most delightful things, though she had to admit, she visited them mainly to see Captain.

"—and the little gown Mama chose is so delightful," Emerald was saying, face effused with excitement. "It is almost as though she is all grown up!"

"She is still a baby," pointed out Amethyst.

The family turned as one to glare.

Emerald flushed. "I-I know that, I just…well, I thought…it does not matter."

"It does matter," said her husband more fiercely than Sapphire would have expected. "Go on, Ems."

Sapphire sighed and took another chocolate. Yes, they were a family in all meanings of the word. Love and fractured arguments. Was that now how all families were?

Another conversation had now started on the other side of the room, and Sapphire turned her attention to it with a grin. It was, perhaps, her favorite pastime: seeing her brother get teased mercilessly by his wife.

"—utter shock of hair, I had to do something about it," Catherine was saying. "You should have seen him!"

"I well know how little Micah enjoyed the barbers," Jasper, the father of the de Petras brood, was saying with a grin. "Why, when he was but ten years old, I had to—"

"Papa!" Micah looked horrified, and Sapphire giggled as she popped another chocolate in her mouth. "Cat does not want to hear—"

"Cat most certainly does want to hear," interrupted his wife with a giggle. "I need more ammunition for our future arguments, of which I assume there will be many! I will need to be entertained during my confinement!"

Micah groaned, dramatically dropping his head into his hands. "I thought you were bored of these stories!"

"Never," teased Catherine, nudging him with her shoulder as she descended into peals of laughter. "Come now, I do not suppose it will be that bad!"

"Oh, you have no idea," came Micah's muffled voice.

Sapphire leaned forward, eager to hear the tale. That was the trouble with being at least several years younger than all your siblings. So many of the stories from their youth were merely fables to her, still so many she had never heard.

"—and the poor man had the shock of his life when Micah bit—"

"I have never bitten anyone else, before or since!" Micah said as that corner of the room laughed raucously.

He rose, moving across the room to pick out a chocolate from the bowl beside Sapphire. She watched with interest as his wife followed him, embracing him from behind as she, too, selected a chocolate.

"Now we both know that is not true," she breathed, evidently for Micah's ears only.

Sapphire flushed red hot as her brother groaned, and she immediately rose from her seat and moved over to sit beside Amethyst.

Well! She was no fool to the ways of love. At least, she had a basic understanding of what occurred between a man and a woman—but the last thing she needed was a reminder that her brother…

It did not bear thinking about!

"You look a little hot, Cousin," said Amethyst awkwardly.

Sapphire breathed a laugh. "Yes, I suppose I do."

Wild horses would not drag a repetition of the words she had just overheard.

"Your brother is rather coarse sometimes, is he not?"

"I suppose he is," mused Sapphire, looking over at her brother as he sat on the sofa with his wife. "But he was a complete disaster before he met Cat, so I suppose we should be grateful she has domesticated him somewhat."

A snuffling noise told her Captain was awake. Sapphire beamed; she adored the dog that had been given to Emerald by Coral's husband as a gift, and she pulled the grumpy dog onto her lap.

"You like dogs, don't you?" said Amethyst, moving away.

"I love them," said Sapphire happily, kissing the mongrel on the top of its head and burying her face in fur before kissing it again. "I have asked Emerald several times if I may keep her, just for a few days you understand, and—"

"And I tell her every single time, she is more than welcome to walk Captain but not to take her home," said Emerald quietly.

Sapphire looked up to see her sister smiling. She had not realized Emerald was seated so close.

"Well, I am not saying I would like to bathe her or clean up after her," Sapphire said with a grin, running her fingers through the dog's fur. "But still. She is beautiful."

"She is a menace," said Emerald with a wry smile.

Sapphire grinned. "We are a perfect match, then."

She looked back at the dog, stroking her gently with her hand and her stub. It was only when she caught Amethyst staring did she meet her cousin's gaze.

"Yes?"

"N-Nothing," stammered Amethyst, immediately looking away.

Sapphire swallowed. She should be used to it now. She knew that she was almost one and twenty and had been out in Society ever since Coral had wed. Well, a month afterward.

Still, there was nothing to inure one from the curious stares of others.

She could not blame them, really. At least, she did not blame the kind ones, the ones who averted their gazes and tried not to focus on the fact that her right arm ended at her wrist. Her stub, that was what she called it, could be easily hidden with gloves, and indeed she did spend almost all her time when in company wearing gloves.

But when at home, when she did not even think about the fact that she was different, she left off the gloves.

Amethyst's arrival had not changed that, but it had made it a little harder.

Sapphire cleared her throat. "She is such a lovely dog, Emerald."

"I would not change her for all the world," said Emerald with a knowing look. "But you cannot have her, she is my dog. Besides, the children adore her so."

"But I adore her so," said Sapphire with a teasing smile, pouting to make herself look even more pathetic.

"And that," came Coral's voice from across the drawing room, "is because you are a child."

The laughter that filled the room was not joined by Sapphire.

Cheeks flushed, heart pounding painfully, she tried to ignore the words that brought such hilarity to her family.

"And that is because you are a child."

She was not a child—had not been a child for such a long time, it was infuriating! No matter what she did, no matter how she tried to prove that she had grown past needing care or babysitting, her family did not seem to see her like that.

Not in the slightest.

"Oh, Sapphy isn't a child, not precisely," called over Micah, a lopsided smirk on his face. "But she can hardly be trusted in Society without a chaperone!"

"I do not need a chaperone," Sapphire retorted.

At least, she tried to retort. She certainly said the words, but it did not appear to matter as no one heard them over the laughter in the room.

Her fingers bunched into a fist, and Captain yelped.

"Sorry, Captain," Sapphire murmured to the dog who leapt down from her lap.

Her shoulders slumped. Was this the curse of every youngest child, to be considered entirely untrustworthy in Society merely because of her age?

Coral had never needed a chaperone! Micah, from what Sapphire could remember, had never had one. Emerald had ventured into Society so rarely, it was hard to remember what she had done.

So it was Sapphire who was forced to attend every invitation with a member of her family. As though she would shame them if left to her own devices!

"Which reminds me, we have not agreed who is to chaperone Sapphy next week," said Micah with a heavy sigh.

Sapphire glared. "I do not need a—"

"Yes, you do, Sapphire," said Opal sternly.

There was little arguing with her mother; Sapphire had learned that a long time ago.

It did not stop her from sticking her tongue out the moment her mother turned away.

"Sapphire!"

"Well!" she said bad-temperedly at her father's shock. "It is ridiculous—I am near one and twenty, more than old enough to comport myself in good Society—"

"And yet you stick your tongue out at your own mother!" Coral teased with a knowing look. "Very elegant!"

Opal turned with an eyebrow raised, and Sapphire had the decency to sigh heavily before she apologized.

"Sorry, Mama," she said grudgingly.

It was too infuriating for words. When were her family going to realize she was a woman now? When would they notice she had her own mind, her own interests—could perfectly well laugh at a gentleman's dull jokes with or without a chaperone?

"It's quite alright, little one," said Opal with a knowing smile.

Irritation flared once more about Sapphire's heart. "Please do not call me that."

"What?" asked Amethyst, looking between them.

Sapphire sighed. Explaining would only make it all the worse! But there seemed little option; it would be cruel to keep her cousin out of the joke, merely because she did not like it.

"It was my pet name as a child—as a *child*, mark you, which was a long time ago," Sapphire said sternly to her siblings who all looked remarkably pleased with themselves.

"Not that long ago," said Micah with a grin.

Sapphire groaned. *One day, they would push her beyond all endurance. One day, she would make them see—*

"It seems like only yesterday that you were born," said Jasper, his eyes misting over. "My littlest little one—"

"Papa!"

What could she do, say to make them see her differently? Was it so impossible—would she have to grow old before they recognized the fact that she had grown up?

"Speaking of little ones," said Emerald, seeming to take pity on her and turning to Catherine, "how does your brother and sister? I heard young John…"

And the conversation moved on.

Sapphire sighed heavily, shoulders slumping as she brought her hand and stub together in her lap.

It was most exasperating, but the trouble was, it did not appear to be changing. It was impossible for her parents, let alone her siblings, to see she was perfectly ready to join the world, dance at balls, strut along Rotten Row, ride in Hyde Park, all the things a woman in Society did…and do it, mostly, without creating gossip.

No, it would have to be something immense to wipe away their assumptions that she could do almost nothing on her own. Something…something scandalous. Something drastic. Something none of them would have ever predicted.

A slow smile crept across Sapphire's face as the kernel of an idea that could be made into a plan crossed her mind. *Now, that might work…*

CHAPTER TWO

March 8, 1814

HE WAS NOT obsessing. Probably. What was the limit to obsession? Was it this far, or further—was it possible to be more obsessive?

James Gresley, Earl of Maltravers—Maltravers, to his friends—groaned and turned away from the door only to turn back immediately, cricking his neck in the process, as he waited for them to arrive.

Well. *Them.* One of them in particular.

He had waited at least half an hour after the invitation had stated arrivals were expected by Lady Romeril, so he would not have to endure being there without the de Petras family, but it appeared they were running even more fashionably late.

Which meant he was left alone with all the ladies of the *ton* who were desperate to secure him for their daughters, and…

"Ah, *there* you are, my lord," said Lady Romeril smartly, striding up to him and practically forcing a glass of wine into his hand. "The party needs to liven up."

Maltravers blinked. "I beg your pardon?"

The older woman, a stalwart of Society who as far as he was concerned, ran the damned thing, raised an eyebrow imperiously. "My card parties are nothing less than a treasure, my lord.

Everyone wishes to receive an invitation, everyone…and so where is everyone?"

Maltravers smiled weakly.

It was an excellent question. Oh, there were a few people there, the sort of people who grasped at an invitation with both hands, who arrived early, eager to speak with everyone, and then had to be gently pushed to the door when it was time to leave.

The sort of people he, and it appeared Lady Romeril, found most dull.

"I would not say no one is here, my lady," he managed, sipping his wine as though that would give him courage. "Mrs. Marnion and her daughters, Mrs. Loughton—"

"Dull people, you mean," said Lady Romeril with a dry laugh. "The sort of people one has to invite, though one has no wish to converse with them."

Maltravers glanced at the door. Lady Romeril's drawing room was large, far more spacious than his own, and it could hold a great deal of people. Its doors—its double doors—were impressive and easily spotted from any part of the room.

Which did not explain why his gaze was so frequently drawn to them.

"Where are they, that's what I want to know."

Maltravers blinked. "I-I beg your pardon?"

Lady Romeril glared. "You know precisely what I mean, you irritating boy. Go and speak to someone, or I shall find you slipping off my guest list."

She strode away to accost someone else, and Maltravers breathed a heavy sigh of relief.

He did know what she meant. *Or more accurately, who she met.*

The de Petras family were not here, and that meant she…

Maltravers swallowed. It was a foolish crush, one he had told himself several times he would outgrow. But no matter how much older he grew, Sapphire de Petras remained the utter image of female perfection in his eyes, and he was nothing without her.

His jaw tightened. *Not that he had her.* Not that he had ever been able to summon up the courage to say anything to her. Not that he had at any point given a hint, any indication…

He could hardly blame her for being dazzled by the charms of more coherent men.

"Ah, my Lord Maltravers. How are you this evening?"

Maltravers blinked. A gentleman was standing before him, one he did not recognize and had even less interest in speaking to.

The door opened. His heart skipped a beat as a woman stepped into the room.

It was not Sapphire.

"My lord?"

"What?" Maltravers said hastily, looking back at the stranger who had accosted him. "Right. Yes, I—what did you say?"

It could not be more evident that the man was offended by his lack of attention, but his title appeared to protect him. It would be a bold man indeed who spoke plainly to an earl.

"I inquired as to your health this evening," said the gentleman more stiffly this time.

Maltravers nodded, then realizing with a lurch of his stomach it was his turn to speak, "Yes—yes, I have good health, I thank you."

He glanced back at the door. They had been invited, had they not? He had not thought to ask Lady Romeril, though she had referred obliquely to them—and he had not even considered asking Sapphire whether she was attending tonight.

Of course she would. Sapphire de Petras would not miss the chance to flirt and chatter with innumerable young men, especially at a card party hosted by her godmother.

A pained smile spread across Maltravers' face. If he did not say something soon, if he did not declare himself…well, Sapphire was popular. There was no keeping men back forever.

"—my lord?"

"What?" Maltravers said blankly, turning to the man who was not taking the hint.

At least, until now. "I see my presence is not wanted," said the man bluntly. "I shall take my conversation elsewhere."

But Maltravers heard not a single word that came out of the man's mouth. Not as the door once more opened and revealed…

A woman. Dressed in blue, a color that had always suited her. From the moment he had realized as a young man that these feelings, these sensations he had when he looked at Sapphire were quite different from those he felt when he looked at…well. Any other woman.

Earbobs of pearls, her favorite, she had mentioned it once at a ball hosted by the Duke of Axwick, and elegant cream gloves that reached her elbows. A figure most elegant, a smile most radiant.

Maltravers swallowed, mouth dry, whole body taut with the effort of not immediately approaching Sapphire as she beamed at her hostess.

How did everyone else not see it? Why did they not realize the image of womanly perfection had just entered the room?

She was not alone. Behind entered her parents, Opal and Jasper, her cousin, Amethyst, who Maltravers still barely knew, and Emerald and her husband. Almost the entire family.

They were all pretty, the de Petras girls, but only one made Maltravers dizzy, senses disobeying every rational thought. One of these days, he was going to slip up and say—

"Maltravers!"

A smile broke across his face as Sapphire approached, pulling him into an embrace that did not last nearly long enough, in Maltravers' mind, even if it was a scandalous thing to do to a gentleman in public.

"Sapphy!" Maltravers managed to extricate himself from her arms, most unwillingly. "You simply cannot embrace gentlemen in public!"

"I'm not," said Sapphire with a grin. "It's only you. What did you say to Lord Anthony Romeril, he looked most unhappy as he left your presence."

"Lord…?"

Sapphire jerked her head to the dull stranger who had attempted to make conversation.

Maltravers sighed. "You know, I have no idea?"

"Letting your mind wander again?"

He tried to smile weakly. It was a constant jest with them, though not one he had ever bothered to explain.

Sapphire teased him that he often permitted his mind to wander, that he would lose track of conversations as his mind thought of other things.

And it was true, in a way. What she did not know was that she was the other things. All of them.

How did one explain to someone who had become, years ago, one of the best friends he had ever known, that you were completely besotted and could never think of another?

"You've gone all blank again."

Maltravers shook his head, as though ridding water from his ears. "No, I haven't."

"Yes you have," said Sapphire decidedly, taking the undrunk glass of wine from his hand and sipping it before handing it back to him, all without a word. "So, who else is in attendance tonight? Anyone interesting?"

He could not help but smile. There was a wonderful closeness between the two of them that he treasured. What other woman would so easily take a sip of his wine without even asking? Who else would he permit to do that?

It would be ruined, if he spoke up.

That was the trouble. Maltravers knew the friendship he had with Sapphire was precious, delicate. If he was to reveal himself—if he was to speak and make it clear he was an absolute fool for her, she would laugh, then she would be shocked…

Then they would never speak again.

Not like they did, at any rate. Not with the easy, comfortable friendship they enjoyed.

And that, Maltravers told himself, *was the only reason he had not yet said anything about his adoration for Sapphire de Petras.*

Not because he was afraid, once he spoke, that she would

leave him. Not because his words stumbled whenever he tried, his heart racing so quickly he could barely—

"Maltravers!"

He jerked back to attention as Sapphire snapped her fingers before his eyes. "Damnit, Sapphy, you don't need to—"

"What did I just say?" she interrupted, eyebrow arched.

Blast. He had not been paying attention, too lost in the crystal blue of her eyes. Others would call them sapphire, of course, but Maltravers had looked into them too deeply and too often to think that.

No, they were crystal. Slightly more green in the evenings, darker blue when she was angry, Sapphire's eyes were crystal that reflected every emotion—

She snapped her fingers before him once more. "Honestly, Maltravers, anyone would think you had somewhere else to be!"

Maltravers grinned. "Nonsense. You know the only place I wish to be is by your side."

Sapphire laughed as she nudged him with her elbow. "Flatterer. Look, there's something I want to ask you—come over here."

There was nothing he could do but allow himself to be pulled over to an empty corner of the room.

The only time he could ever admit his feelings, or at least a semblance of them, was when he pretended he was jesting. Maltravers knew it was foolish.

But then the dream would be over…

"There, now we don't have to worry about being overheard," said Sapphire promptly. "Goodness, that wine was awfully good."

Without saying a word, Maltravers offered her the glass again.

"No, I should probably get my own. Mama will start giving me a lecture about social impropriety again," Sapphire sighed.

"I'll get you one," he said immediately. *Blast. Could he not control himself for one—*

She grinned. "Of course you will. Nice and full, please."

"Does Lady Romeril offer any other?"

The problem with being in love with Sapphire de Petras, Maltravers knew as he pushed his way through the ever-crowded drawing room toward one of the footmen who held a silver platter of brimming wine glasses, was that it was impossible to stop noticing.

Noticing what she was wearing. How she smiled. Her mood, on days when absolute cads mentioned her stub.

And that left him utterly at her beck and call. Did she know, did she have any idea he did not do this for anyone else, that he would never dream of obeying so swiftly if he did not—

Maltravers' heart skipped a beat. He had picked up a glass for her and turned to see…

Sapphire. Laughing, not at something he had said, but at something a tall, irritatingly handsome man had just said to her. It was not Sapphire's normal laugh, he knew that so well he could pick it out of a crowd at a hundred paces. No, this was her awkward laugh. Her, *I have been pinned in a corner by a dullard,* laugh.

It did not require thought, just action. He took another glass from the silver platter. Pushing back through the crowd and paying no attention to the wine spilling down his hand, Maltravers made sure to accidently trip just in the direction of—

"Dear God, man!"

"Maltravers!"

Maltravers straightened up to see Sapphire giggling, and the man she had been speaking with attempting to stop himself from swearing as he wiped wine down his front.

"Oh, dear me, what a shame," he said blandly. "I appear to have tripped."

"You appear to have thrown an entire glass over me, you swine!" spluttered the man, glaring. "Who do you think you are to—"

"Oh, the earl did not mean it, did you, Lord Maltravers?" Sapphire said sweetly.

God, he could kiss her. Maltravers watched the anger drain from the wine-sodden man.

"*Lord* Maltravers?"

"Pleased to make your acquaintance," lied Maltravers easily. "And you are?"

"Needing to go home and get changed, I'll be bound," quipped Sapphire with a smile. "Such a shame to miss your conversation, Mr. Lister. Good evening."

"I…" The man glanced at each of them before gritting his jaw. "Good evening."

Maltravers watched the dripping man stomp away. "What a cad."

"He was most tedious, I assure you," said Sapphire lightly, taking the glass from his hand. "It is truly fortunate Cat warned me of such a man."

A slight flush tinged Maltravers' cheeks, and he nodded without saying a word. Well, he was no fool; he knew Micah had mistresses, had done for years.

What he had not expected was the blighter to marry one of them.

"So, ah, Mr. Lister and Catherine—"

"Never, so I am told," said Sapphire, her cheeks pinking. "Now, I need to talk to you. About something…something important."

Maltravers swallowed and tried not to look too deeply into those beautiful eyes.

Was it possible…could she have guessed? Could she know how he felt, how his heart contracted the moment he saw her? How every word she spoke was precious, how he had kept that stone she had picked up years ago and kept it on his—

"It's strange to say aloud, now I come to it," said Sapphire with a nervous smile.

Maltravers swallowed. *This was it*; the moment he had dreamt of for years, though in true Sapphire style, it was not he who was going to raise the topic, but her. He should have known she would say something first. When had she first fallen for him? Was it possible they could have spent the last year in openness, in happiness—

"I think we should become engaged. Engaged to be married."

For a moment, Maltravers was certain he was having a heart attack.

Or a stroke. Was this not what happened when people were afflicted with such a malady? Their hearing was altered, that was what he had heard.

Because he could not have heard that. Sapphire had not said those words…had she?

"I think we should become engaged. Engaged to be married."

"I…" Maltravers swallowed. *He was not going to lose his head—just because Sapphire did, that did not mean he was going to ignore all decorum!* "I think I must have misheard you, Sapphy. Wh-What did you say?"

Sapphire grinned, that mischievous smile he knew so well dancing across her lips. "I want you to propose to me, Maltravers."

There was no possibility he could have misheard that time. She spoke in such a calm, way…

The room began to spin, and it was all Maltravers could do not to reach out to the wall beside them and cling onto it for dear life as he attempted to take in Sapphire's words.

She could not be serious. But if this was a jest, it was not particularly witty, and she was known for her astuteness.

Was it possible…surely it was not possible that she was serious?

"The trouble is, as you know, my family have not ceased considering me as a child," said Sapphire, as though that explained the entire matter.

Maltravers blinked. "So…so you want me to—"

"Propose, yes," said Sapphire calmly, sipping her wine as the chatter of the card party grew around them. "Preferably in some dramatic way, before them—before many people. Lord, we shall have to think about it."

"We need to—Sapphire, what on earth are you talking about?" Maltravers managed.

She had always managed to surprise him, all the years they had known each other—but this was quite different. She wanted him to…propose matrimony? Before her family?

"It is a brilliant plan," said Sapphire slowly, as though having to describe something very simple to someone very stupid. "It is! They do not see me as anything more than a child, someone who needs chaperoning back and forth—"

That was certainly true. Maltravers always looked forward to the days when one of the de Petras family asked him to escort Sapphire to some invitation or other. And they thought he was doing them the favor!

"—and I thought, well, what is more grown up than getting married?" Sapphire continued. "All I need them to do is see me as—well, a bride, rather than a child. Do you see?"

Maltravers did see. At least, he could see how such an idea could spring into someone as wild as Sapphire's mind, but it still did not explain what on earth they would do…*after*.

His whole body reacted to the thought, and he tried desperately to keep himself calm. The last thing he needed was to continue this conversation with his manhood standing at attention.

"I…well, I do not think this is a good idea, Sapphy," he said gently.

Despite the softness of his tone, Sapphire frowned. "You don't?"

Maltravers shook his head, half wishing he could just go along with the whole charade. To be engaged to marry Sapphire, even as a joke, even for a few days…it would probably be as close as he ever got to the real thing.

"I do not see how it will work," he said slowly. "Why would I propose?"

"Oh, you like me well enough, don't you?" Sapphire said, tapping him on the chest with her gloved stub. "I can't think of anyone else I would rather have propose to me. Certainly not that Mr. Lister, and where else would I find such a good friend who will go along with it?"

Maltravers tried to smile, but it was difficult. No man wanted to be grouped together with Mr. Lister, and any juxtaposition between them was, in a way, a little insulting.

"Where else would I find such a good friend who will go along with it?"

It pained him beyond words to hear her speak like that of him. Just a friend, someone who was malleable and biddable. Was that all he was to her?

"And what about—after?"

"After?" repeated Sapphire, a frown creasing her forehead. "What do you mean, after?"

Maltravers swallowed. "If we were to announce an engagement, would not your family, would not the whole *ton* expect…a wedding?"

For a heart stopping moment, he thought Sapphire would say that they would just go through with it; that they may as well, they meant more to each other than—

"Oh, we'll call it off somehow," said Sapphire dismissively. "Don't worry, I'll leave your honor intact."

Maltravers tried to think. If only desire was not rushing through his veins instead of blood, if only the woman he loved had not just suggested that he propose marriage to her.

As a jest. A trick. A way to make her appear more impressive to her family.

He needed to tell her in no uncertain terms that there was no possibility of—

"Please, Maltravers."

Maltravers' heart twisted as he took in the pleading look of the woman before him. "You don't have to beg, you know."

"I'll get down on my knees and beg if it means you'll go with me on this," said Sapphire with a wry grin. "Please, Maltravers. I am asking you as a friend."

As a friend.

Oh, he wished to be so much more than that, not just a friend and confidante, but a lover. A best friend, a companion throughout life. He wanted to wake every morning with her by his side and traverse the adventures of life with her as his better self.

But if this was the best he could ever have…

A slow smile was spreading across Sapphire's lips, and Maltravers sighed.

"A rather convenient engagement, don't you think?"

She shrugged. "No one will think anything of it."

He sighed. She had him absolutely cornered, and she knew it. He had never been able to deny her anything, that was how they had managed to find themselves in so many scrapes over the years, and this was surely to be the worst. Still…

"Fine—fine! You had better think this through," Maltravers said wearily as Sapphire squealed and embraced him for a second time. "This is a bad idea."

CHAPTER THREE

March 10, 1814

S APPHIRE BREATHED IN the sharp spring air and looked curiously at the pair of ladies.

There was nothing unusual about them. Many ladies chose this particular part of St. James' Park to promenade, the beautiful elegant lawns a perfect splash of color at this time of year, when so few plants were blossoming.

It was just…well. Sapphire had never seen such a bold print on a day gown. Even under the woman's pelisse, it was remarkably fine.

As the two ladies drew level with Sapphire, one of them scowled.

"The cripple is looking at me, Mama," she said haughtily.

Her mother sniffed. "Don't look, Camelia darling."

They strode away, picking up their pace as they passed her.

Sapphire's cheeks burned. They would undoubtedly look scarlet, but there was nothing she could do to quell the heat, it must emerge or she would scream. Perhaps she would scream anyway; perhaps that would make her feel better.

The cheek!

Well, she knew plenty gawped, though in polite Society that was starting to lessen. When one had been out for a year or so,

Sapphire knew she had ceased—in the main—to be a source of entertainment.

But the idea that someone could just say such a—

"I would have said something, if I were you."

Sapphire swallowed, hoping her voice would remain level as her chest tightened. She had been waiting for Maltravers, but now it seemed she would have to suffer the presence of another.

If only she had thought to bring Amethyst, even though it would have been difficult to speak with Maltravers with her cousin here. At least it would have protected her from having to speak to…

Miss Antoinette Goldsmith grinned as she stepped forward. "I see you have been once again insulted."

Sapphire attempted to calm herself and smile, which was difficult. "Yes, though it is no surprise. Some people simply do not have the breeding of others."

A natural smile perked up the corners of her mouth as she saw the impact it had on the gossipy thing. Antoinette Goldsmith; a young woman, close to her in age, absolutely vicious when it came to scandal.

The safest thing to do, Sapphire knew, was to be unremarkable. Then Antoinette would have no reason to do anything, say anything, spread anything that could be injurious to her reputation.

Not that that mattered now. She would be engaged to an earl within the week.

"I'll get down on my knees and beg if it means you'll go with me on this. Please, Maltravers. I am asking you as a friend."

"Fine—fine!"

Perhaps something of the confidence sparking within Sapphire's heart showed.

Antoinette frowned. "What do you have to look so happy for? You were just cruelly cut by those ladies!"

Sapphire shrugged, seeing as she did so how it infuriated the woman. "I suppose I am blessed with far more elevated companions in my circle of acquaintance—ah, here he is."

Her eyes had just caught sight of him over Antoinette's shoulder, and her heart swelled at the relief of seeing him.

Maltravers.

James, she supposed, but it had been a long time since she had called him that. He was always Maltravers, always the tall, quiet, gentle man in the background of her life. Always there, always steady in a way no one else was.

Sapphire beamed. "There you are, Maltravers."

She saw Antoinette's eyes widen as Maltravers stood beside her and bowed.

"You call him—"

"And why should I not?" interrupted Sapphire, a hint of fire curling around her heart.

Well, really! Who was Miss Goldsmith to dictate how she should speak to her friend!

"There is a problem, Miss Goldsmith?" asked Maltravers mildly in that calm way he had about him.

Sapphire's heart swelled with pride. She had chosen well for her scheme; Maltravers would be able to traverse the complexities of Society a great deal better than she could, for all her talk before her family.

Perhaps, in a small way, they were right. Not that she would ever care to admit it to them. But if she'd had a chaperone with her, those ladies would never have made such awful remarks, and she would not have been alone at the mercy of Antoinette Goldsmith…

"No problem, my lord," said Antoinette, curtseying so low Sapphire could see her bosom. She rose and gave Maltravers a beaming smile.

Ah. So that was it, was it? Antoinette wished to catch an earl.

Sapphire almost snorted with laughter. *Marry Maltravers?* It was such a bizarre idea. Even in her scheme to pretend their engagement, she would not actually marry him!

Which reminded her. She did need to conceive of a way to

break off the engagement, in time, when it had done what she planned and proven to her family that she was quite grown up enough to—

"—walk with you, my lord?" Antoinette was saying, fluttering her eyelashes most provokingly. "It is a lovely day, and—"

"No, thank you," said Sapphire decidedly, stepping between the two as impatience blossomed in her chest. The very idea of Antoinette and Maltravers—"Good day, Miss Goldsmith."

Without another glance at the woman, Sapphire marched Maltravers along the path.

"That was not very polite, Sapphy," he pointed out mildly, as though it was a common occurrence and known failing in her character.

Sapphire rolled her eyes. "You would say no such thing if you had been here before. She was quite rude, you know."

"Was she actually rude, or did she just disagree with you?"

She had to laugh, tightening her grip on Maltravers' arm. "If you must know, I am not always offended when someone disagrees with me. They are fools indeed, naturally—"

"Oh, naturally," he said with a grin, tightening his grip on her in return.

Sapphire beamed. Why could not all gentlemen be like Maltravers? But then of course, would she notice just how wonderful he was, if he was one of many? She had never encountered a gentleman with just the right sense of humor.

"In truth, she was rather rude," Sapphire admitted cheerfully, ensuring her smile was fixed. The last thing she wanted was Maltravers to think she had genuinely been affected by anything—or, God forbid, hurt. "But then she followed a cruel pair of ladies who said…said something unpleasant."

"Unpleasant?" Maltravers repeated, staring with a frown as they turned a corner along the path. "Why? What did they say?"

That was perhaps one of the best things about Maltravers, Sapphire thought wistfully. He saw her as…a person. Sometimes he even forgot why people stared as she entered a room.

"Erm…" she said with a laugh, waving her stub before his eyes. "Why do you think?"

It was just a flash, just a moment of uncontrolled emotion on Maltravers' face that was gone before she knew it. If Sapphire had not been looking at him closely at the time, she probably would have missed it.

Rage. Bitter anger, absolute fury. Then it was gone.

"You have to ignore these people, Sapphy," he said quietly, though with warmth in his tone. "They are simply—"

"Ignorant, yes, I know," she said with a sigh. "I know."

How easy it was for him to say. How easy it was for all of them to look at her and presume her reactions should be this way or that way.

"Well, all I can say is that you were right on time," Sapphire said breezily, "or else I may have been forced to say something rather impertinent to Miss Goldsmith."

Maltravers raised an eyebrow. "Oh, Lord."

"Nothing truly disgraceful!" she reassured him with a laugh. "Just…well. She does try my patience rather."

"Well, I wouldn't want to keep my wife waiting," teased Maltravers.

Sapphire rolled her eyes as she laughed. "You really are a fool, Maltravers."

"Only a fool for you."

She laughed again. He truly was one of the best people she knew. He always knew what to say, how to encourage her, force her from any mood she managed to find herself in.

Yes, she had chosen well.

"Speaking of wifedom, though—"

Maltravers snorted. "I do not think that is actually a word, Sapphy."

"Well, whatever." She shrugged. "We will not actually have to get married, you understand? I mean, it is just a ruse. Just a trick on my family."

"And the rest of Society, I suppose," Maltravers said lightly.

Sapphire blinked. She had not actually thought of that, but of course, he was right. If they were truly to ape an engagement, certain things would have to be put in place. An announcement in the newspapers, naturally, banns, the securing of a church…

"Lord, you're right," she said slowly. "I suppose we shall have to plead for a long engagement."

Glancing up, expecting him to make a quip, Sapphire was astonished to see Maltravers was silent, his gaze drifting off into the middle distance.

St. James' Park was busy that afternoon. It was no surprise, it was the first truly dry day in almost a week, and many people of respectability who wished to see and be seen were here, promenading. There were even a few on horseback, those who were undoubtedly worried that their shoes would become damp by the undoubted sogginess of the lawn.

But she could see nothing which might have gained Maltravers' attention so. There was no one before them she recognized, no forbidden duel, no unexpected barouche race.

So why was he so distracted?

"It's just a ruse," Maltravers said faintly.

Sapphire nodded, squeezing his arm in an attempt to gain his attention. "Just a ruse, yes."

"Right." Maltravers took a deep breath, blinked, then turned to her with a brief smile. "Right. So…why are we here?"

"Here?" Sapphire stopped in her tracks and stared at the man who was, after all, almost five years older than her. "James Gresley, do you have truly have no idea?"

For some inexplicable reason, Maltravers flushed.

Flushed! The man she knew would never flush at such a thing, if such a thing had even happened, which Sapphire was not sure had. All she had done was call him by his name, for goodness' sake!

"I-I can't remember the last time you called me that," he said quietly.

Sapphire frowned. "Why does that matter?"

"It doesn't," he said quickly. "It doesn't, I…no, I don't know why we are here."

Sapphire rolled her eyes. And her family thought she was the innocent one, the one ignorant of the ways of Society. Maltravers was an earl! Surely, he would understand why it was absolutely vital to be here.

"We are going to become engaged, correct?"

Why did the man look so uncomfortable? Sapphire could not fathom it, but there was a definite look of discomfort on his face. Perhaps it would be better if they walked. Gave him something to do.

Sapphire pulled on his arm, and the two of them started walking slowly along the path.

"We are…we are going to become engaged," repeated Maltravers, a little breathlessly to Sapphire's mind, which made no sense at all.

What had got into him today?

"And that means…"

Sapphire waited, certain he would understand eventually, but there appeared to be no dawning expression of agreement on his face.

Goodness, when was the last time she had properly looked at his face? Maltravers was just always there, always part of her family gatherings, attending most of the same invitations…

She hardly looked at him in the same way she could not recall the last time she truly inspected her front door. It was there. She knew it when she saw it.

It was only now she noticed just how sharp his jaw was. Walking as she was, she had a rather close impression of it, and she could not recall…was it always like that?

"I don't know what that means."

Sapphire started. "It means," she said, clearing her throat and speaking in an undertone as they passed a gaggle of people walking the other way, "that for anyone to believe this, truly believe this, we cannot just announce the engagement."

"We cannot?"

Was it her imagination, or was there disappointment in his tones?

Sapphire shook her head. She was getting distracted—distracted by Maltravers, now there was a jest!

"We cannot," she said firmly, stepping over a puddle. "Come now, Maltravers, we have been friends for years, and nothing has changed in that time. You think Society will merely accept, all of a sudden, that we have developed feelings for each other? You are the one who called it a convenient engagement, and it must not be seen to be so."

Maltravers glanced at her and said nothing.

Something strange flittered through Sapphire's chest, something hot and cold at the same time.

She swallowed. "A-And that means spending more time together. Even flirting, I suppose. Lord we shall have to think about this."

"Flirting?"

Sapphire shot him a grin. "Can you do that, Maltravers?"

He winked. "That do?"

Their laughter echoed around the park, attracting stares from a few and hushed whispers from others.

Sapphire shook her head ruefully. "I am afraid you are going to have to do much better than that, you know, if you wish to be in any way convincing!"

"Oh, you wound me!" Maltravers placed his free hand over his heart and made a face. "Such cruel words from my future wife!"

"Stop your nonsense," Sapphire said, nudging him with her shoulder. "You'll have to step up your game, Maltravers, if you ever wish to woo me!"

She laughed, expecting him to join her, but for some reason the man had become serious again. What on earth was going on with him? Perhaps he had received unpleasant news, perhaps his estate was taking up far more time than he had expected.

Perhaps the man was just in a dull temper.

"I will see what I can do," Maltravers said in a serious voice, "to win your heart."

Sapphire's laughter faded away. "Well, that's…that's better."

Why had her voice sounded so uncertain? It was ridiculous, she was starting to become as serious as him. He would have to find that levity he so typically enjoyed.

But now she came to think about it, Sapphire could not recall a single moment when Maltravers had used that levity to his own advantage. With the ladies, that was. In truth, she could not recall a moment of flirtation from the man.

"Maltravers."

"Hmm?" he said, smiling, his eyes sparkling in a way Sapphire had never noticed.

"You…you are five years older than me."

"I know," Maltravers said with a wry laugh. "Do you think that will hinder my suit?"

"No, it's just…well," said Sapphire. "I have never seen you flirt with anyone. I had never noticed before, you're just Maltravers, always there, but…well. You are older than me, and unmarried. Not even close to an engagement."

Was it her imagination, or was there a strange shiftiness to his air? Was the man trying to hide something—had there been an engagement?

Something painful lurched in her stomach. It was unpleasant, the idea there would be something about Maltravers like that, so personal, so intimate, that she did not know.

"No, no engagements," Maltravers said lightly. "Other than this one, of course."

Sapphire punched him amiably in the arm. "You know what I mean. There has been no lady who has taken your fancy?"

The man certainly looked shifty now. *To think*, Sapphire thought in wonder, *a secret love affair—Maltravers!*

Her stomach lurched again, and this time it felt different. Angry, somehow. Which made absolutely no sense.

"No one," Maltravers said quietly, smiling. "Or perhaps I

have been flirting, and you have not seen it. Perhaps you are just not looking hard enough."

Sapphire stared. Perhaps he was right; she certainly did not see him, look at him rather, in the same way as others. So who was this mysterious woman then, or women perhaps, he had been flirting with?

"You're jealous."

"No I'm not!" Sapphire spoke without thinking, eager to immediately defend herself from such a ridiculous aspersion. "Why would I be jealous?"

"I don't know," said Maltravers lightly. "Aren't you?"

Sapphire swallowed. She was, in truth, which was ridiculous. Maltravers was not her brother, nor her husband that she should feel such things. In truth, he could flirt with whoever he wanted, marry whoever he wanted.

But the idea of Maltravers with a wife; a woman he would be closer to, with whom he would share all his secrets, all his thoughts, all the thoughts he now shared with her…

It was an unpleasant thought.

"Well, here we are then, giving the gossips something to remember when we announce our engagement," said Maltravers briskly. "Come, let us sit on a bench."

"Just a little too close," said Sapphire impetuously, grinning.

When they sat, he was pressed up against her in a way that was most unusual. Sapphire was astonished to find how warm it made her.

"I think Coral will have the most dramatic reaction to the announcement."

Sapphire snorted. She would not have permitted herself to make such a disgraceful noise in front of anyone else. "Coral will claim to have a hand in it somehow, as is her way."

"That is Coral."

"And you know, I had a great deal to do with her own happy match with Edward, you know," Sapphire said with an arched eyebrow.

"Poppycock."

"It's true!" Sapphire said, giggling in mock outrage. "No, I swear it, I made her come on a walk with me in Hyde Park—I think it was Hyde Park, it may have been here—"

"Your story becomes less believable with every detail you concoct, Sapphy," Maltravers said with a grin.

She smiled back. There was no one else she could speak like this with, no one else she wanted to. There was something about him; though he was more of an age with her brother, even when they had been young, it had been the two of them who had been drawn together.

"I swear it, I goaded her into flirting with him—and a terrible job she did, I must say," said Sapphire in a stage whisper. "I was there, I tell you, when he offered to help her find the perfect husband." She sighed happily. It was strange, looking back. She could never have guessed just what that comment would lead to. "And I suppose he did, in the end."

Maltravers shifted on the bench beside her. "I've got a question for you, Sapphy."

"Oh Lord, you cannot ask me here," said Sapphire hastily, looking wide eyed.

"That was not actually the question I was going to ask," he said with a dry laugh, "though noted, you wish for something more impressive than a damp bench in a park."

Sapphire placed a hand on the wood. "Is it truly damp?"

"Why me?"

She blinked. It was not a question she understood. *Why him? Why him…what?*

"Why ask me to be a part of your little scheme?" Maltravers explained, obviously reading her confusion. "This pretend engagement, this engagement to make your family sit up and take notice…you could have asked anyone. Why me?"

Sapphire shrugged. She did not have to think about the answer. "Why not you?"

Why was there a slightly crestfallen look in Maltravers' eye? "Why not me?"

"Well, it is a large task, obviously," said Sapphire pragmatically. "Putting up with my family, trotting out with me to invitations, bearing with the terrible loss of my affections—"

"Sapphy—"

"So, I needed someone I could trust. Call it...call it a favor after a lifetime of friendship," she said cheerfully.

But for some reason, that cheerfulness was not reflected in her friend. Quite to the contrary, Maltravers looked a little dejected, his spirits low, his shoulders slumped.

"I see."

"Do you?" Sapphire said, her smile fading as she reached for Maltravers' hand, taking it in her own. "Because there is no one else I would trust with this, Mal."

A strange sort of smile quirked Maltravers' lips. "Mal?"

"It's just a nickname," Sapphire said hastily, "I do not have to—"

"I like it." He spoke calmly and squeezed her hand. "I like it."

Warmth spread across Sapphire's chest at his smile as the tension within him seemed to melt away. Well, she did not understand where it had come from, but that did not appear to matter anymore. As long as it was gone. As long as she had her Maltravers back.

"In that case, Mal," she said primly, "we have an engagement to plan."

Chapter Four

March 15, 1814

"AH, THERE YOU are!"

Maltravers grinned. Well, it was difficult not to when someone greeted you with such joy, such genuine pleasure at your arrival.

There were so few people in his acquaintance who did, still fewer who were, in a strange way, like…well. A mother to him.

He clasped Opal de Petras's hands as he stepped into the parlor. "And an absolute pleasure it was to be invited, Mrs. de Petras."

"Oh, you and your nonsense," smiled Opal with an arched eyebrow that reminded him of her youngest daughter. "You are practically family, dear boy, you need not wait on an invitation into this house—I am sure Sapphire does not wait on such ceremony with you!"

She laughed, elegantly releasing her hands from his as she strode to the other side of the room. "I said no, Beryl, Captain is very welcome here but not on my sofas!"

Maltravers smiled at the scene. Emerald's two children were running about the place utterly uncontained—they had not inherited their mother's shyness—with their father chasing after them, evidently mortified at the casual way they treated their grandparents' home.

"Beryl, no! Topaz, what did I say about—"

Micah was laughing in a corner, his wife absent. When was her confinement to begin? Maltravers could hardly keep track, in truth, but it could not be long now. She had been showing rather obviously for some weeks now.

Coral was absent, as she so often was at these things. More important matters elsewhere. Maltravers could not understand what it was to be a lady and the heir to a family; he never had much choice in being his father's heir as the only child.

Sapphire sat laughing in a corner, evidently greatly amused by her nieces' antics.

"There's a chair you haven't clambered over!" she teased them, goading them into more mischief as only an aunt could.

Maltravers' heart ached to be part of such a moment. Just the de Petras family and himself. Was there a greater honor? Was there anything better than a family afternoon tea?

He would not know.

His smiled faded. Would his parents have hosted such events, would they have invited the de Petrases to afternoon tea? If his mother had lived, would he have had siblings; brothers and sisters to amuse himself with, to play with the de Petrases?

A strange thought occurred to him, making his stomach lurch. *If he'd had siblings, would he have forged so close a bond with Sapphire?*

And the moment passed. Sapphire had risen to her feet, snorting with laughter in that way she never permitted herself to do when in company, and grinned as she approached him.

"The rabble grows ever louder," she said conversationally.

Maltravers grinned. "Your nieces are terrors."

"Wonderful, isn't it?" Sapphire laughed. "I think I would have been quite put out if they had been dull."

"Beryl, no!"

"I think Em quite has her hands full," continued her sister blithely as they watched Emerald lurch forward to prevent her eldest daughter from clambering up the window sill. "Though I imagine Micah will soon join her, in time."

There was a strange look on her face at those words, a tone Maltravers had never heard within her before. It was almost…serious. A very unnerving thought.

"Sapphy?"

Sapphire blinked, then smiled. "Nothing, I was merely lost in thought for a moment. Now I come to think about it, what are you doing here?"

Maltravers' smile faded. There was no malice in her words, no irritation—just genuine surprise. He was not sure which was worse.

"I…well. I asked your mother if I could be included in your next family afternoon tea," he admitted quietly as the raucous around them drowned out their voices.

Sapphire was staring blankly, and he had to force himself not to step forward and immediately kiss those inviting lips.

How could she not see it? Was she so blind that she could not see his attraction to her, his devotion—the way he wanted to be with her and no one else, incomparable to all others—

"Why on earth would you do that?" Sapphire asked as one of her nieces started bawling in the background. "It's chaos here!"

It certainly was chaos, but it was the chaos of family, something he had never experienced. With his mother passing when he was born and his father only a decade after that…he had never known the glorious noise of a family.

"Because," he said, taking a step closer and wishing he had any sort of gumption to take her hand in his, "I am courting you. Remember?"

Sapphire's crystal eyes gazed up, wide and uncomprehending. Goodness, she was so close. Perhaps closer than was appropriate, but nothing in Maltravers willed him to step away.

Step away from Sapphire? Step away from happiness, joy, the sense that everything was right with the world, that at any moment she would come to her senses and—

"Courting?" she repeated, then understanding dawned. "Oh, courting!"

Maltravers had to laugh at the blank look which had so quickly been transformed. "Goodness, I am astonished you did not remember. This is your scheme, if I recall."

That was the trouble with Sapphire. She was able to get underneath one's skin in a most irritating way that made it impossible to stop thinking about her.

The moment they had parted after their conversation in St. James' Park—a conversation rife with opportunities to tell her the truth, none of which he had taken—Maltravers had been unable to stop thinking about her.

Thinking about what this false courtship would look like to the world, what it would look like to the de Petras family. What it would feel like, playing court to a woman he had loved for so long. It was difficult to know when it began and he ended.

"You need to remember, Sapphy," he said quietly, stepping closer so his arm brushed up against hers. "I would hate you to…forget, let us say, that this is merely a ruse, and begin to think there was something truly in it."

For a heart stopping moment, Maltravers forced himself to hold her gaze. Did she understand? Could she comprehend what he was trying to tell her?

She certainly looked astonished, her eyes wide, those kissable lips slightly parted in astonishment…then she laughed.

"My word, you have been practicing!" she said cheerfully. "Excellent flirting, you almost had me there for a moment. Well done."

Maltravers forced a smile. "Thank you. I do my best."

She held his gaze for a moment, only a moment. It was probably only about a second, Maltravers told himself later, but at the time it felt like forever. Just the two of them in a room, the rest of the world falling away, as his heart beat faster and faster and—

"Catch her!"

Instinctively, Maltravers reached out and halted the rebellious little girl from rushing past him into the hall.

He leaned down on his haunches to look the girl in the eye. "Beryl de Petras."

She colored, evidently unaware someone other than family was in the room. "Yes?"

Maltravers grinned. There was little of Emerald's spirit in her, that was true, but she had her eyes, her coloring. Her way of flushing when in the spotlight. She was most definitely Emerald's daughter.

"Are you listening to your grandmother?" he said sternly.

Beryl's shoulders drooped. "No."

"Good," said Sapphire, kneeling beside him. "I never do, look how cheerful I am!"

"Sapphy!"

The reprimand rang out from all sides, and Maltravers could not help but laugh. *There was only one Sapphire de Petras.*

"Go on with you," he said genially, turning the child around and releasing her.

He smiled as he watched her run, instinctively, to her mother, and straightened up with a wistful thought in his heart.

Sapphire had forgotten. For just a moment, just a hint of a moment, she had forgotten their plan. *What did that mean?* Did that mean it was so routine in her mind that she had forgotten his role in it…or was it something more than that? Something more exciting?

"Ah, Mr. Levy! How delightful to see you."

Maltravers blinked as Opal stepped past him and Sapphire to the door, where a gentleman he did not recognize was standing awkwardly.

"How good of you to come!"

"Who is that?" he muttered to Sapphire, who looked stony and pulled up her gloves.

"That," she said darkly, "is my suitor."

Maltravers' jaw dropped. *Sapphire's suitor?* He had not heard of any suitor, none of the family had mentioned…

And of course, he reminded himself sternly as the gentleman smiled and was smiled at by Opal in return, there was no reason the family would inform him of such a thing. *He was not family,* he thought darkly. He may feel as though he was, but he was not.

He was just a friend of the family. He had no right to be informed when his Sapphire—

"I say suitor, it's my mother's idea," said Sapphire with a groan. "She is determined to cast handsome gentlemen in my path to see if I take a liking to one of them."

Maltravers' stomach lurched. "Handsome?"

"Well, don't you think he is?" she said nonchalantly, nodding in the gentleman's direction. "You do not have to like a person to find them attractive."

Maltravers swallowed. *And what was he supposed to say to that?*

Oh, this was impossible. The feeling he had enjoyed when he had first arrived was dissipating rapidly; he was not the special one who had been invited to a de Petras afternoon tea. He was one of two, perhaps more.

"And this is my daughter, Sapphire," Opal said magnanimously as she approached with the gentleman beside her. "Sapphire, this is Mr. Levy."

Maltravers watched as the man bowed, his eyes lighting up at the sight of the beautiful woman before him, and Sapphire curtsied, nothing but plain indifference on her face.

But was it indifference? He and Sapphire had never spoken about matrimony, not seriously. What was she seeking—was it only a handsome face? Could she be so easily swayed by a man with a fine features and good conversation?

Had he, in fact, missed his chance because he had not spoken?

"Oh, and this is James," said Opal with a laugh. "I am sorry, James—the Earl of Maltravers. You know someone for so long, I am sure you understand, Mr. Levy, you quite forget the proper introductions for these things."

Maltravers nodded while Mr. Levy bowed. Which was right, of course. He was the one with the more impressive title—a title at all—and therefore he was given precedence.

It had nothing to do with how the cad was looking at Sapphire.

"—so lovely to see you this afternoon, Miss de Petras," the blaggard—for blaggard he surely was, Maltravers had no doubt—was saying with a charming smile.

Maltravers had the horrendous impulse to punch him in the jaw. He managed to contain himself, clasping his hands together behind his back.

The absolute last thing he should be thinking of doing was attacking some poor blighter merely because he talked to Sapphire and enjoyed her company. He would be fighting off every man in the street if he started doing that.

"Thank you, Mr. Levy," said Sapphire blithely. "What a surprise to see you. My mother did not mention you at all."

Maltravers stifled a smile. Sapphire had a wonderful way of speaking very politely, very precisely, yet at the same time, wounding quite brilliantly.

Mr. Levy's smile faded somewhat. "Yes. Well."

Opal shot a warning glare at her daughter, inclined her head to Mr. Levy, and wandered to the other side of the room.

"I wonder, Miss de Petras, whether you will be attending Almack's next week?"

Sapphire's smile was weary, and Maltravers' heart soared. *She did not like him.* He was handsome, at least in her own words, though he could not see much to be impressed by, yet she did not like him.

It was foolish to feel so triumphant. It was not as though he had won her hand.

"I will, sir," said Sapphire shortly.

Mr. Levy grinned. "In that case, may I have the honor of—dear God, what happened to your hand?"

Maltravers stiffened. He looked immediately at Sapphire, who had colored but did not move her arms, and continued to look directly at Mr. Levy.

"Why, whatever do you mean?" she asked calmly.

"Y-Your…your hand…" spluttered the man. "God!"

Maltravers did not have to think. There was no need for thought about filth like this.

"Come on," he growled, grabbing the man by his collar and wrenching him toward the door.

"Maltravers!"

"What is—Sapphire?"

"My word!"

Maltravers ignored the cries behind him. He had no need to ask permission from the family; he knew full well that if Jasper had been here, or if Micah had heard the man's idiotic words, they would be doing precisely the same.

"I only asked a question!" cried Mr. Levy as Maltravers forced him along the hall and toward the front door. "Can't a man ask a question?"

"A man might, a gentleman would have far more discretion!" spat Maltravers, pushed beyond all endurance by the cheek of the man. He wrenched open the front door and pushed the man through it, his surprise and shock making him stumble down the steps. "A gentleman would have considered asking Mrs. de Petras in quiet, in private, a gentleman would have got to know the lady before even thinking to ask such a person question, and a gentleman, a true gentleman, would not have thought it any of his business to ask in the first place!"

With great satisfaction, Maltravers slammed the door in the man's astonished face.

His blood was boiling, shoulders heaving, chest tight, heart pounding, and for a moment, Maltravers lost all vision, so great was his anger.

What was wrong with people? They thought merely because Sapphire was different, they could just demand information, ask questions about her she had no need to answer!

It was abhorrent. It was disgusting. It was—

"You know, you're doing a very good job of this," came a

quiet voice.

Maltravers looked up. Sapphire was leaning against the doorframe of the parlor, a smile on her face.

He tried to take a breath. Yes, he was filled with rage at the impropriety of asking someone that, but that did not mean he had to make a complete fool of himself.

"What do you mean?" he asked in a jagged voice.

Sapphire's smile widened. "Well, pretending to be courting me. That is precisely the sort of thing a man wishing to win my hand would do."

She stepped into the hallway and closed the door behind her, looking at him in silence.

Maltravers swallowed. He stepped forward, knowing in this state he certainly should not be anywhere near her, intoxicating woman as she was, but he could not help it. He had to make sure she was unharmed by the encounter.

He had to be close to her.

"I will not permit—no man, no person should ever..." Maltravers cleared his throat. Somehow, he had come much closer to Sapphire than he had intended. So close in fact, that as his chest heaved with the breath he was so desperately attempting to take, he was almost brushing up against her breasts.

He was not going to think about her breasts. Damn.

"People like that, people like him," he said quietly, "should not be permitted your time."

"It was only a question."

"You do not owe answers to anyone," he said emphatically. Could she not see how perfect she was, how important she was, how the world could go hang itself for all he cared? "You do not need to justify yourself to anyone, you know that, Sapphy."

"I am not ashamed," Sapphire said, lifting up her chin in that proud way she always did when she felt quite the opposite.

Maltravers smiled, and knowing he would probably regret it the moment he acted on the instinct, raised a hand and cupped her cheek. *When was the last time he had touched her? Weeks?*

"I know," he said softly. "I know."

She looked up at him, trusting, completely comfortable with him. Maltravers' breath caught in his throat. If only she could look at him like this all the time, always with that warm and open expression.

As though she was just waiting for him to kiss her.

Which he was not going to do. Even if every part of him was crying out to touch her, he would not permit himself. Even if he was leaning, just ever so slightly, closer to her…

"Mal?" she whispered, her gaze still fixed on his.

Maltravers suddenly realized what he was doing. He was about to kiss Sapphire!

Dropping his hand immediately, he took a step back. "I just don't think people should be so blatant in their treatment of you as a curiosity."

"P-People are curious," Sapphire said.

Why had her voice caught there—was it because of him? Or more likely, Maltravers reminded himself, was it because of that cad Mr. Levy?

"I'm not."

Sapphire breathed a laugh at that. "That's because you know me. You're not fascinated with me because you already know all my faults."

Maltravers tried to smile but knew better, in that moment, to attempt to speak.

Because he was fascinated by her. He had been fascinated with her the first moment he had ever met her, as children; and not because she was different, but because…well, she was *different*.

Different from anyone else he had ever met. Bolder, and braver, saying the things people always thought but never verbalized, laughing at the world's foolishness while others merely went along with it to keep on the right side of good Society.

She fascinated him. She mesmerized him; sometimes he

would hear the applause at the end of an opera, when he joined the de Petras family, and realize he had not taken in a single note because his entire being had been fixed on the woman next to him.

A woman who evidently had no idea what she did to him.

"Yes," Maltravers said weakly. "Your faults. Numerous as they are."

"Oh, Mal."

And suddenly Sapphire launched at him, embracing him tightly, her breasts pushed up against his chest, but far more importantly, her head on his shoulder.

Maltravers could not help it. He brought his arms around her, tightening his grip on her, as though if he just clung on long enough, she would never leave him. He breathed in that scent that was pure Sapphire, and closed his eyes, losing himself in the moment.

"I am so glad to have you as my friend," came her whispered words in his ear.

Maltravers' heart twisted painfully, but he kept embracing her, kept holding her for when would he ever be gifted such a wondrous moment again?

"Me, too," he said quietly. "I mean, I am glad to have you as my friend."

Sapphire snuffled a laugh, and he tightened his arms around her, his hands on her waist, the tears she had repressed as Mr. Levy had spoken now finally let loose.

This was what he wanted. Oh, to kiss her, touch her, yes, all of that—but Maltravers wanted more than that. To be a part of her life, to stand by her, to be her protector, to be the one she ran to when hurt and ran to when she wished to celebrate.

To be her partner in everything.

Maltravers swallowed. *This was only going to get more complicated.*

Chapter Five

March 20, 1816

"Oh, don't be such a—"

"If you call me baby," muttered Sapphire in as violent a whisper as she could manage as they stepped into the lights of Almack's, "I will scream."

Fiery irritation had hardly left her chest from the moment the de Petras family had stepped into the carriage.

Well, not the entire family. Catherine and Micah were too close to her confinement, Sapphire had been informed, and Emerald and Coral were too busy with little ones of their own to bother about such gaiety.

Sapphire smiled, despite her frustration, as she took in the sights, sounds, and smells of Almack's. But she and Amethyst? They were quite ready to be entertained after a dull day sitting at home, looking out at the rain. She would even accept a few more stares than normal if it meant seeing walls that were not her own.

Besides, Almack's was…well. Not as tedious as home, that was for certain. Vouchers appeared to be given out to anyone these days, Sapphire thought as she spotted a few people she did not recognize.

And the worst of it was, she had been plagued by teasing the moment her father had stepped into the carriage.

"I was not going to say such a thing!" said Jasper, holding his hands up in mock surrender as he saw the glare on his daughter's face. "I was only going to say—"

"Well, don't," said Sapphire sharply. "I am tired, I tell you, sick and tired of always being the baby, the little one—"

"You are the youngest," pointed out Amethyst fairly as she took a glass of wine from a footman as he passed.

Sapphire glared at her cousin. Was it not her position to support ladies of a similar age? Should they not be standing together against the tyrants that ran this family?

Her heart softened, despite herself however, as she saw her mother's smile. It came from a good place, she knew that. She was fortunate to have a family so loving and interested in her welfare.

Even if that meant a little gentle ribbing.

But why could she not be like Micah or Coral, teased about a great number of varied things. Why, when it came to her, was it always about her age?

"Topaz is the youngest," Sapphire said tartly, a false smile on her face. "Did you not think to retrieve a glass of wine for me, also?"

Amethyst's eyes sparkled with mischief. "A little one such as yourself should not—"

"I wish you would desist," said Sapphire, the rage she had managed to calm spiking.

Her mother was gesturing to Lady Romeril a few yards away.

Sapphire smiled. Though she did not completely understand the full story, having not been born when it happened, she knew their family had a great deal to thank Lady Romeril for.

Why, if it had not been for her support at her parents' scandalous second marriage…

Well. Perhaps they would be denied vouchers to Almack's, despite the alacrity with which they were distributed.

"I really should go and speak to her," Opal said to her husband as Sapphire glowered at her cousin genteelly sipping her wine. "It has been weeks since—"

"I am sure Amethyst and Sapphire can behave themselves," said Jasper with a wink.

Sapphire did not smile. She was almost one and twenty, for goodness's sake! Old enough to be married, to run her own home and be her own person—just because she had not yet decided on a gentleman, that did not mean they could treat her like…like a child!

"I can chaperone the little one," said Amethyst with a grin.

Try as she might, Sapphire could no longer hold it in. She was not going to permit her family to treat her like—like a little one!

"I will have you know," she said as stiffly as she could manage, "that I am being courted by a fine gentleman and am likely to be very soon *engaged*. To be married."

She looked up triumphantly. Well, they would have to take a little more notice now; an engagement was something the entire family would come together for, would celebrate.

Her mother tutted under her tongue. "Oh, she has gone to speak to Mrs. Howarth—I think it best, you know, after her daughter's…unfortunate entanglement with Micah, that I do not approach this moment."

"A wise decision, my dear," nodded Jasper.

Sapphire could have screamed. What did they want? Why was an announcement—a pre-announcement, really—of an engagement still not enough to make her mother see her differently?

Did she have to drag the gentleman over here to make it believable?

Now she thought about it, from this vantage point, she could not see Maltravers. Where on earth was he? He had promised he would be there in plenty of time, to ensure they could make a scene.

A positive one, of course. Sapphire stifled a smile. She wanted to be gossiped about for all the right reasons, not all the wrong ones.

"I said, Mama," she said clearly, her voice a little louder perhaps than it needed to be, but apparently that was the only way to get any attention in her family, "that I am being courted by a gentleman of the highest—well, not quite the highest nobility, but pretty *damn* high—"

"Sapphy!"

"—and am soon to be engaged," plowed on Sapphire, ignoring her father's outrage.

Opal blinked. Then an indulgent smile crept across her lips. "Of course you are, dear."

And without another word, she stepped toward Lady Romeril.

Sapphire stood, mouth open. *Was that it?* Was she to be so dismissed, so summarily disbelieved that even her own mother did not wish to inquire further to ascertain whether this mysterious gentleman existed?

Amethyst was laughing. "You should see the look on your face!"

"Oh, be quiet," said Sapphire bad temperedly.

It was not her cousin's fault. It was all of them. None of them even comprehended the idea of a gentleman liking her enough for a courtship, let alone marriage. If only—

There he was. Maltravers.

Sapphire smiled, perhaps naturally for the first time since she had entered Almack's, at the sight of the tall and well-dressed gentleman stepping into the ballroom.

And about time, too. She would not have been forced to endure such mockery from her family, surely, if he had been here. Though now she came to think about it, most of the teasing she was subjected to was dished out while he was there.

It was a damned shame. *Damn.* Damn damn—

"Miss de Petras, Miss Sapphire," said Maltravers with a bow. "Mr. de Petras, always an honor."

Sapphire curtseyed as was expected, along with her cousin, and tried not to take the etiquette of Society personally.

When Emerald had married, she had awaited eagerly the opportunity to be Miss de Petras. Not Miss Sapphire, the baby of the family. Miss de Petras, the eligible lady of the family.

But with Amethyst's arrival, just a few years older than her but that was all that mattered, she was relegated once more to Miss Sapphire.

The little one.

"Maltravers, always marvelous to see you," said Jasper warmly. "Tell me, how—"

"Maltravers can answer your questions later, Papa," said Sapphire suddenly, struck by an idea that she simply had to carry out now. "Come on."

"But—"

"Sapphire!"

She ignored the calls of her father and cousin, grabbing Maltravers by the hand and pulling him to the side of the room. Loud chatter surrounded them, the very best of the *ton*—and a few others—filling up the ballroom fast.

Sapphire swallowed. No, there were too many people. It was entirely possible she could be overheard; she would have to find somewhere else.

"Here, perhaps?" she said impetuously, striding over to a door with Maltravers' hand still clasped in hers.

His hand was warm, his fingers steady. Reliable. Strong.

Sapphire blinked. *Why had she thought that?*

She needed to focus. Opening the door and pushing the confused earl through it, Sapphire closed the door behind them and sighed as she leaned against it.

"Yes, this is perfect."

"Perfect?" Maltravers looked around. They appeared to be in a storage room of some kind; wooden chairs were stacked all against one wall, and there was a table with empty vases on the other side. In truth, it did not leave much room for them.

But that did not matter, Sapphire told herself. They only needed to talk, it was not as though they needed space for anything else.

"You know, if anyone finds us here, in all honor I will be forced to ask for your hand," said Maltravers quietly.

Sapphire grinned. "Well, that would be one way of enacting our plan, wouldn't it? A very convenient engagement."

"Except I would have actually have to go through with the wedding," Maltravers pointed out.

Her eyes widened. "Lord. Yes, I hadn't thought of that. We'll have to be quick then."

That was the trouble with her plan, wasn't it? Their engagement had to be realistic enough to get the *ton* talking, to make her family treat her as someone equal to the rest of them…but also easy enough to slip out of.

Well, she could worry about that later.

Sapphire was about to say what she had intended to say the moment she had seen Maltravers enter Almack's, but hesitated when she saw the expression on his face.

It was…strange. Like nothing she had ever seen before, at least not on Maltravers' face. She had seen that expression before, somewhere, that vague, unfocused look, an intensity that burned.

Her stomach swooped most unexpectedly.

"M-Mal?" she said softly.

Maltravers blinked, his eyes focused, and when he spoke it was in a perfectly calm tone. "You must have had a reason to pull me into what appears to be a glorified cupboard, Sapphy."

She smiled. *There was the Maltravers she knew.*

"I need you," she said seriously, "to propose as soon as possible."

His mouth fell open. "Sapphy!"

"What?"

"You cannot just—"

"This was the plan," Sapphire reminded him, stepping away from the door and smiling as she grew closer to him. "Remember? We pretend to court, you propose to me, I get to flaunt the engagement to my family—"

"Lovely," said Maltravers dryly.

She grinned. "You know what I mean."

His smile lingered on her face for a moment before he dropped his gaze. For some reason, and Sapphire was not entirely sure why, her chest tightened.

Which was ridiculous. This was Maltravers. She had known him her entire life!

He was…well. More brother than gentleman.

"So…do you mean now?" he said quietly.

There was a slight note of panic in his voice, and she giggled as she shook her head. "No, silly—but soon. My family is becoming absolutely intolerable, and if I am to put up with them one minute longer—"

"Did you ever wonder whether it is they that put up with you?"

"Nonsense," Sapphire declared, grinning mischievously as her friend pointed out something that was probably true. Not that she would ever admit it. "They treat me like a baby, Mal, you have seen it time and time again. I'm sick of it."

"And you," said Maltravers taking a step toward her, so they were only a foot away now, "are no baby."

Sapphire nodded, but found to her confusion that she did not appear to have enough breath to speak.

It must be the dust in the room. There was no other explanation for it, she doubted whether anyone bothered to clean in here. Why, there must be months, years of dust!

That was why her throat was choked as she looked up into Maltravers' eyes and saw…saw something.

"Explain to me," he said softly, "how this is going to help you?"

Sapphire rolled her eyes. "It's obvious."

"Not to me."

How did he do that? Speak so softly and yet with such power, such authority?

It truly was infuriating.

"I will explain it as briefly as I can, then we should probably return to the ballroom and dance, or something else that…that courting couples do," said Sapphire as calmly as she could manage.

Maltravers said nothing. He just nodded, his complete attention focused on her.

Which was wonderful. *When was the last time*, Sapphire wondered suddenly, *someone had paid complete attention to her? Just her, no one nor nothing else.*

In a family with so many siblings, nieces arriving and Captain still scampering round the place, there was always something else going on, something else to look at, listen to, laugh with—or at.

But not with Maltravers. When she was with him, he was truly listening.

Sapphire swallowed. The room felt smaller, somehow. It was the lack of light, there was only one candle in here after all. That had to be it.

Dizziness overwhelmed her, just for a moment.

Then she collected herself. "You see, an engaged…an engaged woman has to be listened to. Has to be spoken to with a modicum of respect, do you see?"

Maltravers was looking at her closely. "I see."

Sapphire straightened up, throwing back her shoulders in an attempt to ground herself. She was only having a conversation with Maltravers, of all people!

"Yes," she said, a little more certainly. "They will have to treat me as an adult, as a full member of the family when I am engaged. And I cannot put up with this nonsense much longer, I need you to…propose."

Maltravers nodded seriously, though there was a glint of mischief in his eyes. "Soon."

Sapphire smiled. "If you don't mind."

Though her words were entirely innocent, there was something strange in the air. She could not understand it.

It was just Maltravers, yet he did not look like Maltravers.

That was, he was certainly Maltravers, Sapphire thought wildly, *but he looked different, somehow. Unlike himself.*

There was a power there, a strength she had noticed before but never really examined. As he stood before her, just inches away, she was struck by just how very…masculine he was.

Which was a foolish thing to think.

Because he was always like this. Always tall, always calm, always a presence in any room he was in. Perhaps it was because they had never been in a room quite this small. Alone.

And then a look passed across his face that made Sapphire's mouth fall open.

Concern. Regret. Perhaps even discomfort.

He did not want to do it. Propose to her, that was. Despite him agreeing to the plan days ago, Sapphire saw in that moment that Maltravers was still not completely decided on going along with it.

Most unfortunate.

"Maltravers," she said quietly, not looking away, "you…you are going to propose to me, aren't you? For the ruse?"

Maltravers took a deep breath, then nodded curtly. "For the ruse. Of course."

Sapphire hesitated. "Good."

And it was good. It was a brilliant plan. Sapphire was remarkably pleased with herself that she had concocted such a thing. After all, no one would disbelieve such a thing, they had known each other for so long. He was an eligible bachelor, an earl…

Their engagement would not just be something small noted in a corner of a newspaper, something her mother would undoubtedly pay for.

No, this was going to be news. Not just in the gossip sheets, but actual news. She swallowed, her stomach turning over most unhelpfully. Actual people would read about.

He wasn't just Maltravers. Her Maltravers. He was the Earl of Maltravers, and his marriage, any engagement that he entered into…it would be talked about.

"You have to be certain about this," Sapphire said impulsively.

"Whatever do you mean?"

"You know what I mean," she said, smiling at his gentle voice. It always calmed her, no matter the situation. "I mean, you may—you may have another lady you are thinking of proposing to, and our scheme—"

"Might ruin my chances with her?" There was a dry smile dancing across his face, one that was too knowing, in Sapphire's opinion. "Do not worry yourself, Sapphy. When I come to propose, the woman I offer marriage to will completely understand this little jest."

Sapphire's eyes widened. This woman, whoever she was, evidently had a most forgiving nature. She was not certain she would wish for her future husband to be so entangled.

"You are sure of that?"

"Very sure. But as I will not be offering her my heart anytime soon, I do not think we need to worry."

Sapphire nodded, though curiosity flooded through her. "So, there is a lady, then?"

"Sapphire," he said with just a hint of warning.

She grinned. "You can't blame a girl for asking."

And then Maltravers did something most unexpected. He took her hand in his, and without hesitation, he took her stub in his other hand.

Sapphire gasped. She was wearing gloves of course, as any lady at Almack's would, but still, the sensation was remarkably intense. He was holding her—not her hands, obviously, but…

This was far more intimate than anything she had ever experienced. Even her sisters did not touch her stub; not that she had ever forbidden them from doing so, but it had become an unspoken thing between them. It was a part of her that did not get touched.

But now it was. Now, as Maltravers looked deep into her eyes, and Sapphire found her breath catching in her chest, her whole body felt as though it was being touched. As though fingers were lightly brushing across every inch of her skin.

Maltravers, James Gresley, the man she knew perhaps better than any other in the world…he was looking at her like—

"I am willing to do this for you," Maltravers said quietly, his dark eyes flashing as he spoke, no hint of a smile on his face. "Do you understand, Sapphy? I do this for you."

Sapphire swallowed. This was all getting far too serious for her liking, yet she had no desire for this moment to end. To ever end, which made no sense. Why would she want to spend the rest of her life standing in a store room?

"Y-Yes," she managed to splutter, swallowing in an attempt to strengthen her voice. "I-I do understand. Thank you."

Maltravers smiled. He let go. "In that case, I suppose we should return to the ballroom and cause a little gossip so that our future engagement does not come as any surprise!"

Maltravers strode past her and opened the door, only then saying quietly, "Sapphy?"

Sapphire blinked. The entire room had spun there for a moment, and it was only now starting to right itself. *What was going on?*

"Sapphy?"

"Hungry," said Sapphire, turning on her heels to smile at Maltravers.

He blinked. "I beg your pardon?"

"I am hungry," she said firmly. *Yes, that must be it.* "I must eat."

Maltravers made a face. "What, here? At Almack's?"

Sapphire groaned, relieved that normality had somehow been restored. "Oh Lord. I shall starve, then."

CHAPTER SIX

March 21, 1816

MALTRAVERS LOOKED BLANKLY at the box that had been handed to him. His hearing seemed to be gone, a vague swooshing and swirling, like the sea. All he could see was the box.

Someone cleared their throat. "Would his lordship like me to open it for him?"

Maltravers blinked. Everything came into view; a formal room lined with a delicate wallpaper and green leather lined chairs.

The bank manager smiled. "When did you last retrieve this from your vault?"

It was a difficult question. Maltravers had never done such a thing before; when his father had placed the family jewels in this box, he had only been a boy. The precious things were put away in the bank—where they belonged, his father had always said—and there had been no need to retrieve them in the long intervening years.

Until now.

"A while," Maltravers managed to say with a brief smile.

This whole thing felt rather strange. Typically, his butler or steward came to the bank, Maltravers himself had never been. Oh, he had been treated with the utmost respect, naturally, the bank manager coming out to deal with him personally.

It was always good manners to deal so with an earl.

But now the box was before him, Maltravers found he had no wish to open it. When he had last seen it…

"Here," said the bank manager, a Mr. Norton, smoothly. "Allow me."

Before Maltravers could say anything, before he could ask the man to leave him while he gathered enough courage to look inside it—*which was ridiculous, why would a man need courage to open a box?*—Mr. Norton leaned forward.

He opened the box.

It was about a foot square, and now it was open, Maltravers could see that there were many little, smaller boxes inside. One caught his eye immediately.

It was about an inch across on all sides, made of blue velvet, a gold M monogrammed.

Hand shaking, loathing the fact he was being forced to do this before an audience, Maltravers reached out, took the small blue velvet box out of the larger mahogany one, and opened it. There, nestled in the blue velvet, was…

"My lord?" Mr. Norton sounded nervous, as well he might. Maltravers had not said a word. "Everything is to your liking, my lord—everything is as you would expect?"

Maltravers nodded without saying anything. Well, he had determined to play his part properly, and the contents of this box would certainly aid him in doing so. Still, he could not help but wonder whether he had made a terrible mistake, coming here, retrieving it. If word got around, before he spoke to Sapphire—

"You will speak of this to no one," he said smartly, shutting the box with a snap and placing it in his pocket as he looked up expectantly at the bank manager. "Do you understand?"

"Of course, my lord," bowed Mr. Norton, evidently thrilled to be part of a secret with an earl. "And is there anything else you wish to retrieve from that box? There are many wonderful things within it—"

"And how do you know that?" snapped Maltravers.

He knew he should not react so strongly, knew it was ridiculous to be so blunt—

Mr. Norton's face had become stern. "Because we have a ledger, my lord, and I take the security of my bank seriously. Very seriously indeed."

Maltravers swallowed. He needed to leave. "Of course. Thank you, Mr. Norton, that will be all."

It took only ten minutes to leave the bank, but it could not come swift enough. When Maltravers stepped onto the pavement, newly damp from a recent rain shower, he found his chest tight and a heavy weight in his pocket that was entirely disproportionate to the size of the box.

It was a marvel, really, that something so small could weigh on him so.

Well, he had it. Awkward though he may feel in walking about with it, he had what he came for, and that was the main thing. The afternoon was drawing in swiftly. He would have to return home, ensure Reeves, his valet, would have time to dress him.

Maltravers' jaw tightened. Before the evening.

Reeves was indeed delighted to be dressing him for another ball.

"So wonderful to see you out and about in Society more often," he chatted away as he perused Maltravers' large cravat collection, attempting to decide which would go best with the blue and gold waistcoat he had already chosen. "And I must say, I think the Penshaw Ball is the height of the Season's excellence, there is nothing better…"

Maltravers allowed him to witter on. He had nothing to contribute, after all. His attention was wholly focused on his jacket, lying on the chair before him. He must remember to take it with him. The box, that was.

A fine fool he would make of himself if he asked Sapphire de Petras the question that he had, in truth, wished to ask her for a few years now. It was not perhaps to be asked in the manner he had hoped for, of course…

"It's just a ruse."

"Just a ruse, yes."

Maltravers' jaw tightened.

"You appear worried, my lord," said Reeves nervously.

Maltravers smiled genially at his valet. A loyal man, one who had been raised from the position of footman just a few years ago, and was still very eager to please.

"I am, Reeves, but it is of no matter," he said quietly, laying a hand on the man's arm. "I am truly impressed with your choice. Thank you."

The man beamed. "Well, blue is such a wonderful color on you, my lord, it is hardly difficult to—"

"Yes," the earl interrupted. He needed a few moments of silence, of relative peace and calm before he left for the Penshaw Ball tonight. Before he took the next step of their scheme; before he asked a question that—

"An important night tonight, my lord," said his valet quietly.

Maltravers caught his eye. Had there been gossip amongst the servants—had one of them seen where he had gone, perhaps what he had brought back with him?

But there appeared to be no special knowledge in his valet's eyes; instead, there was an understanding, a sympathy perhaps at the taut muscles in his jaw, the tense way he had held himself as he was being dressed.

He tried to smile. "A very important night, yes. Perhaps…perhaps the most important night of my life."

His gaze flickered over to the hidden box in his jacket once again. To think, if anyone had told him even a few weeks ago he would soon be proposing matrimony to Sapphire—a question, moreover, he was absolutely guaranteed to receive an affirmative reply…

Well, he would not have believed it. He could hardly believe it now.

"Will that be all, my lord?" Reeves was remarkably perceptive.

Maltravers nodded. "Thank you."

The servant bowed, quietly leaving the earl alone in the dressing room.

Without waiting a moment after the door snapped shut, Maltravers strode over to the jacket and pulled out the velvet box. He opened it, slowly, the candlelight glittering in the precious jewel that was found within.

A sapphire. A large, square sapphire surrounded by a circle of diamonds, all enclosed in the finest of gold.

Maltravers swallowed. He would have to hope she liked it. That it fitted.

After not seeing the engagement ring of his mother for so many years, the precious stones were dazzling, almost blinding his eyes. And in just a few hours, it would be sitting on the hand of the woman he loved.

"You're a fool, Maltravers," he muttered to himself, snapping the box shut and placing it in his waistcoat pocket. "A fool, if ever there was one."

The Penshaw Ball was always popular. The man had great taste, not that Maltravers had ever seen him—the duke himself, it appeared, rarely bothered to be with his guests the entire ball.

But it did not matter. Maltravers could see viscounts and their ladies, military generals and foreign princes, all mingling about together as he stepped through the resplendent hallway and into the ballroom.

And this, he thought dryly, *was why he would never host his own ball.* Goodness, the place was absolutely packed, and doubtless with a few people who would be duller than ditchwater. And—

A face. Dark chestnut hair, a blue gown made entirely of the finest silk, from what he could see, a winning smile that made his heart lurch so painfully it was impossible to continue.

Maltravers came to a halt. There, just inside the ballroom, leaning against a pillar with the nonchalance of a gentleman, was Sapphire.

She was loitering near the door, his heart told him immediately, *waiting for him.*

And then, only then, did the reality of what they were planning to do rush through him, overpowering him, making it almost impossible to breathe let alone see.

They were going to be engaged. Engaged, to be married.

True, in her heart it was nothing but a clever scheme. Sapphire did not look at him as a gentleman, Maltravers knew now, but as a friend, someone she could never love in that way. She would not have asked him, surely, for this great favor if she had any intention of considering him, truly, for her hand in marriage.

Yet that had not stopped him, had it? Maltravers knew himself better than he would have liked, knew that in truth it had probably spurred him on. After all, if he could not claim her heart, her real love, her false love was perhaps the closest he was going to get.

Maltravers' heart contracted painfully as all these thoughts rushed through him. He was of half a mind to turn around, leave Penshaw's ball, ensure he did not make the mistake of bearing his heart, his very soul to a woman who would not understand it was all true...

But Sapphire caught sight of him. Her smile broadened, reaching her eyes as it had not done before, and she waved.

If only his stomach would behave, Maltravers thought wretchedly as he smiled and waved back. If only she had been waiting there for him because she loved him. Because she could not bear to be apart from him.

But it was all part of the plan they had concocted.

"Mal!"

Her cry carried across the ballroom; the musicians had not yet started, with guests still arriving, and heads turned to see what outrageous woman had been so bold to yell at a ball.

Maltravers shook his head with a wry smile as Sapphire pushed past people in an effort to reach him. There was only one Sapphire.

"Excuse me—sorry, I need to get over there and see—excuse you, I do say!"

Sapphire's words of gentle reproach and apologies as she pushed past people in the ever-increasing crush of guests floated over their heads, and Maltravers had to laugh.

She was incorrigible.

"There you are," Sapphire said with a sigh of relief as she reached him. "There!"

She punched him very lightly on the arm.

"I must protest at this outrageous treatment!" Maltravers jested, joy rushing through his body at even her slightest touch.

Which was ridiculous. His heart should not be pounding, he should not be worried everyone here at Penshaw's Ball had seen them. Because that was all part of the act, was it not?

At least, Sapphire's act. He had never had to act less in his life.

"Well!" Sapphire punched him lightly again.

"What is all this for?"

She grinned. "I have been waiting for you forever."

His heart melted. Oh, if only he could reply with the same words, Maltravers found himself thinking, while conscious he needed to maintain the dignity of an earl at the ball.

If only he could admit, when they were alone, that he had been waiting for her. Waiting to realize that she cared for him, or at the very least, that he cared for her...

"I am hardly late," he pointed out. "There are still many people arriving, and—"

"But they are not you," Sapphire said simply.

Maltravers knew his smile was getting silly as he looked into the beautiful smile of the woman he loved. He undoubtedly looked much like a lovesick whelp, but he could not help it. Who could help it, with such a woman before them?

"You need to do it soon."

Maltravers blinked. So lost had he become in his thoughts that for a moment, he had thought Sapphire had asked him to do it soon. *It?* What on earth was she talking about?

Then his eyes focused, his heart skipping a painful beat in his chest. "Ah."

"Ah is not what I want to hear, Mal," Sapphire said with a laugh. "Honestly, anyone would think you were having second thoughts about this!"

Try as he might, Maltravers could not keep his expression calm. A passing footman provided an excellent distraction; taking a glass from the platter in his hands, Maltravers tipped back his head and swallowed the entire glass of wine.

"Maltravers!" hissed Sapphire, pulling him past a pair of gentlemen arguing about politics and a young lady attempting to gain the attention of a gentleman on the other side of the room. Only when the two of them were standing by the pillar, where she had been waiting—a place that gave them a little more privacy, though privacy at a ball was always lacking—did she speak again. "You are having second thoughts!"

"No, I'm not," Maltravers said quickly.

His hand moved automatically to his waistcoat pocket. The box was still there.

"Yes, you are!" she insisted, eyes wide. "You agreed, you said—"

"I know what I said," Maltravers murmured.

It was so frustrating. Perhaps he should never have agreed; perhaps it had been a mistake to tell the woman he loved that he would propose, when it was only to trick her family.

A trick he, in truth, was still a little at sea about.

"Mal," Sapphire said, and he was astonished to find that she was, perhaps for the first time in her life, serious. "You promised."

Maltravers swallowed. He had promised. It was a promise easy to make at the time. Who would not wish to propose matrimony to Sapphire de Petras? Who would not leap at the chance to propose to any woman, in truth, if one knew one was guaranteed a positive reception?

But as he looked at her, heart aching, Maltravers knew there was no way back. He had made his decision, made it the moment she had asked him. There was no getting out of it now. Even if he wanted to, which he did not.

"I will…I will choose my moment," he said quietly.

Sapphire arched an eyebrow. "And is that moment going to be tonight?"

Maltravers stifled a grin. "You could always propose to me, you know."

Her laughter attracted the attention of a fair few gentlemen around them—all of them, Maltravers noticed irately, looking rather impressed.

"Don't be daft, Mal," she said easily. "Come on!"

Slipping her arm in his, evidently unconcerned it was the arm with her stub, Sapphire gently steered Maltravers across the ballroom. He did not understand why at first, but then—

"Ah, Sapphire, I had wondered where you had got to—but now I see you went to retrieve James," said Opal, a wide smile on her face. "How are you?"

"Very well, Mrs. de Petras, I thank you," said Maltravers formally.

Almost the entire family was here, though that was no great surprise. An invitation to the Penshaw Ball was not one to be ignored lightly.

Jasper stood beside his wife, their daughter Emerald just beside him—hiding mostly in her husband's shadow, Maltravers had to admit, but then that was no great surprise from the shyest of the de Petrases.

Coral, on the other hand, was elegantly wafting a peacock feather fan, gaining more attention than usual, her husband was chatting away to Micah, who looked a little anxious.

"No Mrs. Catherine de Petras tonight?" asked Maltravers genially.

That was it. A little conversation with the family, a few moments of pretending everything was normal—

"Her confinement began in earnest this morning, after she revealed how exhausted she was," said Opal with a wry smile. "It always overtakes one the first time."

"Cousin Micah did not wish to come this evening," said Miss Amethyst de Petras in a conspiratorial whisper that carried across half the ballroom. "But she persuaded him."

Maltravers caught a quick frown on Micah's face before he calmed himself and returned to conversing with his brother-in-law.

He stifled a smile. The de Petras family never enjoyed gossip, particularly when it was about them. At least, Sapphire did, but the rest had no taste for it.

"I was just saying what a splendid ball this is," said Sapphire pertly, nudging Maltravers. "Was I not?"

"Y-You certainly were," agreed Maltravers, hardly sure why it was important that he agreed but doing what he was told, at any rate.

He would do anything for her. Anything. It was pathetic, he knew, but when one loved another so vibrantly, so passionately as he loved Sapphire...was that why his heart was beating so frantically, why his mouth was dry?

"Yes, so many *exciting* things happen at balls, don't they, Maltravers?"

Maltravers widened his eyes at Sapphire, but she merely grinned. Did she have to be so obvious? He would choose his moment.

"Oh, I do not think you will have to worry about any excitement, little one," said Opal cordially. "You're barely out of the nursery as it is!"

Sapphire's cheeks flared red, gaze dropping to her feet—then glanced at Maltravers.

He swallowed. He took a deep breath.

This was his moment, he knew, but now the moment had come, he felt strangely distant. As though he was standing with a great pane of glass between them all, sound dimming, movements slowing, heart pounding loudly in his chest. Could they hear it?

"Sapphire," he said.

Sapphire immediately turned to him. "Yes?"

Her eyes were wide, her face expectant, and Maltravers knew he could do nothing to disappoint her. He would do whatever it took, ruin his good name if that was what was required to break off this false engagement in the future…

If it made her happy.

"Sapphire, I-I must ask you something."

"Yes?" Sapphire said, stepping closer to him.

Slowly, very slowly, ignoring the gasps of those around him and the dropped jaws of the de Petras family, Maltravers lowered himself onto one knee before the woman he loved, fumbling fingers reaching into his waistcoat pocket.

Vague words meandered into his ears, all spoken by the de Petras family.

"He's not—"

"He is!"

"Surely he would never—"

"Is that a ring?"

"Sapphire de Petras," Maltravers said quietly, not taking his eyes from hers. "We have known each other for many years, and the last few have been torturous, my affection for you unspoken, and for all I know, unrequited. I should wait, I know, but I cannot any longer. It would make me happy—so happy—if you would consent to be my wife."

He opened the velvet box.

Gasps rang out in the ballroom and then silence, broken only by the heavy thumping of his heart and the shallow breaths of his chest.

Maltravers looked at Sapphire. She was smiling, a gentle blush coloring her cheeks. She was playing her part well, and it was a part, he had to remember that. He could not forget that this scheme was concocted by her, not him.

"I-I will marry you, Maltravers."

A roar of celebration rose up in the ballroom, led by astonished joy from her family.

Maltravers hardly heard it. She had said yes. It was not a true yes, of course, and he must not lose sight of the ruse, but still. *She had said yes.*

Rising to his feet, he took advantage of the situation—one he would never be able to do again—and pulled her toward him.

For just a moment, her eyes widened in shock, Sapphire evidently thought he was about to do the unthinkable and attempt to kiss her—but she sank into his embrace warmly, her fingers nestled in the nape of his neck, and Maltravers could have wept for joy.

"Oh, James! An engagement, an engagement for Sapphire!" Opal's voice appeared to be beside herself. "And to James, too, what a wonderful—"

"Never thought you would do something so foolish as that!" said Micah as he clapped him on the back. "Sapphire!"

Sapphire pulled away from Maltravers' arms all too soon and was swiftly surrounded by her congratulatory family. Her cheeks were flushed, eyes bright, and she laughed merrily as Maltravers silently pushed the sapphire ring onto her finger.

There. It was done. He had proposed, and she had accepted. And she looked…happy.

Maltravers' heart twisted painfully. Strange. She looked so happy, while he felt empty.

CHAPTER SEVEN

March 30, 1814

E VERYTHING HAD GONE according to plan—as she had known
it would.

"But what do *you* think, Sapphire?" her mother asked, embroidering on the sofa.

Sapphire beamed. *What did she think.* An excellent question, one that had hardly ever been asked of her before a few days ago, and now?

Now she was included in every familial discussion, her opinion sought on all matters, and as far as she could recall, she had not been called 'little one' at all.

It was a marvel. It was a triumph!

She should have pretended to get engaged years ago.

"At the end of the day, it's important we have your opinion," said Jasper seriously from the small desk pushed up against the wall, as he puzzled over some paperwork brought over from his shipping business. "Where is Micah, I told him to be here—"

"Here I am!"

Sapphire giggled as her older brother crashed into the room, skidding on the polished floor and causing her cousin to jolt with surprise. Over a year now, and still Amethyst was unaccustomed to Micah's wild ways.

"I told you to be here an hour ago," said Jasper with a wry smile.

"And I told Catherine the very same thing," Micah said breezily, inclining his head at his mother as he strode across the room and pulled up a chair to sit beside his father. "And it turns out, your opinion did not matter much to her!"

"How very fed up is she?" asked Sapphire, placing her book down as she giggled.

Micah rolled his eyes. "If I survive this, I shall be a very fortunate man."

Their laughter rolled around the room. Her brother would never have made such a quip before his youngest sister until recently—very recently. As recently as she acquired herself a betrothed, in fact.

He had always considered her far too young to listen to "his nonsense", as he put it, but now...apparently, she had aged a great deal in the last few days.

"I can well remember it," Opal was saying, "the heaviness at the end—"

"All she can really do is sit and sigh," said Micah with a laugh. "I have told her she can do whatever she wants when the baby is finally here—"

"And she promptly told you that she always did?" quipped Jasper.

Sapphire smiled as conversation continued. She had done it. And Maltravers had said it would not work! That just went to show how much he knew; it was a perfect plan, and they had delivered it to perfection.

Now all she had to do was bask in the glory of—

"Sapphire, what do you think of this bonnet?" Amethyst was seated on the sofa near her and offered the straw bonnet she had been amending with a scandalously bright pink ribbon. "Your Mama thinks it gaudy—"

"That is because it is gaudy," said Sapphire's mother.

"It is not gaudy, Aunt Opal!" Amethyst protested, and to

Sapphire's great surprise, leaned closer to her and spoke in a low whisper. "I know you could persuade her to approve of such a design, she says she will not permit me to wear it when we—"

"It is rather shocking, Amy," said Sapphire with a gentle smile, and saw her cousin smile at the pet name. "You honestly could not pick another color?"

"Mr. Rivers said it was the height of fash—"

"Mr. Rivers is a haberdasher, and his business is to sell," called Opal across the room. Sapphire stifled a smile; her cousin had not lowered her voice sufficiently. "And if you ask me, he overordered that disgusting pink and was desperate to get rid of it!"

Amethyst's shoulders slumped. "Truly, you think so?"

"I know so," came the pert remark from across the room.

Sapphire leaned forward and took the bonnet. It truly was the most ridiculous thing she had ever seen. "I shall wear it for you," she said boldly, stomach lurching at being seen in such a thing. "Now I am an engaged woman, I can wear anything I want. Perhaps I shall create a fashion for it, Amy, lead the way for you!"

"You'll certainly create a stir," muttered Micah, grinning as he glanced at his sister.

Sapphire stuck out her tongue. *Incorrigible man.*

"Well, I suppose if you think it suitable, Sapphire," Opal said with a heavy sigh. "Wear it. See what reaction you get. Perhaps you will start a fashion."

Sapphire's mouth fell open.

She must have misheard her mother. There was no possibility those words had actually come from her mouth, it was an impossibility.

"Well, I suppose if you think it suitable, Sapphire. Wear it. See what reaction you get. Perhaps you will start a fashion."

When was the last time her mother had permitted her to do anything wild and rebellious; anything that could be in any way construed as mischievous? But now, for some reason, it was perfectly acceptable.

A slow smile crept across her face. The only answer, of

course, was that she was now engaged. Engaged to be married. Engaged to be married to an earl!

It was a complete falsehood, but there was no reason her family should know that.

Amethyst took back the hat with a grudging smile. "Well. I hope you look well in it."

If Sapphire was not mistaken, her cousin was rather put out that it would not be her who could first wear the monstrous bonnet, but in her mind that it was all to the good. After all, she had no desire to attract the attention of a gentleman, did she? She had Maltravers.

Her cheeks burned, only for a moment. *Well. Not precisely.* She did not have Maltravers; he never would have said those marvelous words—she really must remember to congratulate him—if she had not essentially cajoled him into doing so.

Where had he got those words, anyway? They were most ingenious, she could have almost believed them, if she had not known the truth.

"I want you to propose to me, Maltravers."

"Show me the ring again."

Sapphire blinked. Amethyst was smiling, a little nervously this time, and her gaze was fixed on the fourth finger on Sapphire's hand.

"What?" Sapphire said blankly.

Her cousin nodded toward her hand. "The ring, you dolt, the ring! Show me."

"Oh! Oh, yes," said Sapphire, remembering too late that she was wearing the thing.

She stretched out her hand, and the sun's attempts at spring pouring through the parlor's windows made the jewels sparkle, throwing sparks of light, rainbows and blue, across the room.

"Oh, it is so beautiful, so elegant," murmured Amethyst, leaning close to the ring as though she could not take in its splendor unless she was two inches away. "To think, Maltravers chose this ring for you, love in his heart as he did so!"

Sapphire smiled. "Yes. Yes, I suppose he did."

She looked in turn at the ring, which had not left her hand since Maltravers had placed it there at the Penshaw Ball. It was a beautiful ring. She had never seen a sapphire so large, and when combined with the diamonds, it made a splendid sight. The gold seemed to deepen the blue of the stone, and even from a distance it was difficult to miss.

Tilting her hand, the sparkles it created scattered around the room.

"Are you trying to blind us with that bauble, Sapphy?"

Sapphire grinned at her brother's complaint. "You're just sore you didn't choose such an elegant ring for Catherine."

"You had better not show her that thing," Micah jested back as their father chuckled. "She'll be at me for an improvement!"

"And to think, you will be a countess!" Opal said, laying down her embroidery as though she simply could not help herself. "A duchess, a marchioness, a countess, and—"

"A Catherine," said Micah dryly.

Sapphire's stomach tightened with the expectation of a row. Micah had always been a little sore that he would not be the de Petras heir, and without a title—

"And a Catherine," said Opal, smiling at her son. "My favorite daughter-in-law."

Jasper snorted. "Your only daughter-in-law."

Sapphire laughed along with the rest of her family, heart singing. This was what she wanted, parity, equality with them, that was all. To be treated as one of the family rather than a child who had managed to sneak into the room.

It was well worth it, whatever the cost would be later. Which reminded her, she had not yet entirely worked out how she would entangle herself from this engaged…

Maltravers would know, she thought. He always had a solution.

"—remember when she was born," Opal was saying, looking at her youngest fondly. "And I remember thinking—"

"What a pretty baby," Micah and Sapphire chorused.

Amethyst giggled as her aunt flushed. "Have I told that story before?"

"Only about once a week, my dear," said Jasper mildly. "Come, Micah, you must concentrate—we must choose, spices or passengers, it is a great decision…"

"We will of course have to wait until Catherine's child is safely here before we have the wedding. We may have to wait a whole month!"

Sapphire's head jerked to her mother. "I beg your pardon?"

Opal was smiling serenely. "I said, we should wait until Catherine's child is here before your wedding to young James. I mean, it would hardly be fair for us to—"

"No, not that bit," said Sapphire, her heart in her mouth. *She had misheard, surely she had misheard…* "The other bit."

Opal frowned. "We—We may have to wait a whole month."

"A whole month?" Sapphire repeated in horror.

A whole month? Only four weeks—was that the only grace she was to receive until she would have to end this charade and lose the precious respect she had only just gained?

No, she had expected a much longer engagement than that; months, perhaps a whole year, if she could wangle it. There had been no expectation that the wedding would occur within a month—at least, not in her mind!

It appeared, however, that her mother had other ideas.

"Well, now you and James have finally revealed your mutual affection—and what a wonderful proposal, indeed," said Opal, "I thought you would be eager to…well. Marry."

She gave her daughter a meaningful look.

Sapphire flushed and looked at her hand and stub clasped together in her lap.

Her mother had accosted her only yesterday, determined to have a conversation with her that was most unnecessary on two fronts.

Firstly, because she had absolutely no intention of going through with this false engagement to Maltravers—not that she could admit that to her Mama, of course. And secondly, because she knew full well what her mother was attempting to tell her, and she did not need to hear it from her mother's lips!

"Coral has already explained—you do not need to…I know," Sapphire had said wretchedly in that awkward conversation yesterday. "Honestly, Mama, you don't have to—"

"I just thought, with your engagement now announced in the papers," Opal had said, just a hint of discomfort, "I would be no mother if I did not explain to you—"

"I know," Sapphire had said firmly, cheeks burning at the idea that her mother was going to attempt to explain lovemaking to her! "Really. This conversation is at an end."

Opal had not attempted to raise it again, for which Sapphire was supremely grateful, but it appeared she was alluding to it now.

"Eager," her mother repeated, eyes wide, "to *marry*."

Sapphire's flush was not disappearing; if anything, it was only increasing in temperature and therefore presumably in color.

So, her mother believed her and Maltravers so eager for each other that they may cross one of the most important boundaries of Society and…make love! It was almost laughable, if it were not so embarrassing and ridiculous. She and Maltravers, do anything of the sort! It was most absurd. She could not imagine anything so foolish!

And for some reason, one she could not fathom, a memory surfaced in her mind. Her conversation with Maltravers in the store room they had found in Almack's. The way the walls had seemed to close in, how close Maltravers had stood to her. Her sudden realization that he was very much a gentleman, and not just a gentleman, but a man.

A man.

Had she ever stood so close to a man before? Sapphire could not remember any occasion. Was that why her breath had been short, because it had been so strange?

"Well, I for one will thank you for extending your engagement, just a little."

Sapphire's head jerked up. Her brother was grinning, leaning over the back of his chair to look at her, while their father shook his head in wry exasperation.

"You would?"

Micah nodded. "The longer I have to accustom myself to having a baby in the house before I have to see my little sister go off to become a wife, the better!"

"Well, there you are, Mama," said Sapphire, grasping at the excuse as though it would save her in a storm. "If Micah would like the wedding put back until the autumn—or perhaps even the winter—"

"Micah de Petras, you do not get to dictate the plans for your sister's wedding!" Opal scolded good naturedly.

"He doesn't get to dictate anything," teased Sapphire.

"No, that's Coral's job!"

Amethyst's words brought a sudden and rather discomforting end to the laughter.

Sapphire saw the pain on her brother's face, the awkward upset on her cousin's, and smiled ruefully. If only Amethyst learned there were some things one simply could not jest about; it would make the whole thing much easier. As it was…

"Yes, I suppose that is right," said Micah quietly before turning back to his father.

Sapphire cleared her throat but could think of nothing to say. Amethyst had returned to her bonnet, cheeks pink, and Opal had picked up her embroidery.

Sapphire did not pick up her book. Instead, she held her hand before her, fingers outstretched, and looked at the large engagement ring that was upon it.

An engagement ring. *Her* engagement ring.

It was strange; the entire time she and Maltravers had plotted this idea, they had never discussed a ring. She had rather presumed Maltravers would not bother to go to so much trouble. It was a false engagement, after all, not a true one. It was not as though she would have kicked up an almighty fuss if she did not have one.

But he had proposed with it. As though he had the thing lying around.

Sapphire smiled wistfully. As though he had chosen it with her in mind the moment she had suggested the trick, then kept it.

Though of course, there was a possibility he had it for another woman.

The thought sent a jolt of pain through Sapphire's chest. Maltravers and another woman? Impossible. He had never showed any particular preference to anyone in the past, she would have noticed.

Wouldn't she?

"Ah, James!"

Startled, Sapphire looked up to see the man on whom her very thoughts were wending appear before her. A lopsided grin on his face and an easy manner as he inclined his head to her family, his eyes eventually alighted on her.

"Sapphire," Maltravers said quietly.

Sapphire's heart skipped a beat.

Which was only natural, after all. He was a dear friend of hers, almost a part of the family! Far more a part of the family than Amethyst, not that she would ever admit to as much aloud, of course.

"Oh, James, how wonderful it is that you will become part of the family!" said Opal with a smile, patting the seat beside her. "To think, if your dear father could see us all now…"

Sapphire's stomach lurched as Maltravers moved around the room to sit close by her mother.

Goodness, she had not thought of that. Of course, Maltravers had no family, his parents had both died. In a very real way, and a way she had not particularly noticed until now, her family was his family.

All he had.

"—saying to Micah, we will have to wait for the wedding

until Catherine's confinement is over, I am sure you understand," Opal was saying as Maltravers nodded. "We must have the whole family together!"

He continued nodding, his gaze flickering in her direction and smile widening.

Sapphire smiled back, warmth flooding through her body. She could have chosen anyone; well, not precisely anyone, but there were surely gentlemen out there in Society who would appreciate a little notoriety which an engagement would bring.

But she had chosen Maltravers, and had chosen well. He knew her family, understood why the plan was so perfect—and besides, no one else would have understood the jest.

"—could not agree more, Mrs. de Petras," he was saying smoothly with a charming smile. "Why, we could even push back the wedding until the winter if—"

"That is just what Sapphire said!" Opal looked over at her daughter, then at the man she presumed would soon be her newest son-in-law. "Remarkable, that I never saw it before, the affection between the two of you, but then of course these things do happen so naturally…"

Sapphire's smile faded. It would be difficult when they broke off the engagement. Her mother would be upset, true. *Blast*. She would have to think of a way to do it without anyone getting upset.

"—want to give her away!"

"There are few English traditions this family has, my dear," Jasper was saying firmly, "and that is that the father gives away the bride."

"But you gave away the first two!" Opal was saying, a teasing smile on her face. "I think it only fair that—"

"They always bicker like this, don't they?"

Sapphire blinked. Unnoticed, Maltravers had moved to sit beside her. His comforting presence was like a balm to all her worries, all her fears. As though her concerns had simply melted away.

"Yes, they do," she said happily. "Rather wonderful, isn't it?"

"It is indeed," said Maltravers seriously, though there was a flicker of mischief in his eyes. "I hope to be able to bicker so well with my future wife."

Sapphire grinned. "I shall do my best."

He did not frown, though no smile appeared. In fact, Maltravers' expression did not change.

But something did. The intensity in his eyes, perhaps, the way he was looking at her, an intensity that near took her breath away.

He had never looked at her like that before.

CHAPTER EIGHT

April 3, 1814

"—HAVE TO GO?"

"Unfortunately, yes, I have a short visit into the country to make tomorrow and leaving at first light will make it much easier to return the same day," Maltravers said with a smile. "But please know, Mrs. de Petras, I leave your company only under protest."

He grinned as he saw Micah pretending to vomit behind his mother.

"You always were kind, James, and you are welcome here any time," she said as Maltravers inclined his head to the rest of the family party.

It was, in truth, a shame he had to leave. There was always good fun to be had at a de Petras dinner; laughter, jokes, more companionship than Maltravers experienced elsewhere.

His country estate required a meeting with him and some tenants, and there were some things one could not do through a letter.

A day that would take him far from Sapphire.

"Oh, Mal, you don't have to go," she said, a look of disappointment on her face that made his heart contract. "And I was just about to beat you, too!"

"You were about to do nothing of the sort," Maltravers protested as Coral laughed on the other side of the card table. "You filthy cheat!"

"Now, it is rather bad form to accuse the ladies of cheating," said Robert with a grin, his wife Emerald smiling, too. "Even if they are—"

"Robert—"

"I suppose I was getting a little help," admitted Sapphire freely with a grin.

Maltravers had to admire her. Any other woman would have colored, protested, argued until she was blue in the face and still refused to accept she was cheating.

Sapphire just came out with it. She truly was spectacular.

"A little help!" Coral looked absolutely outraged. "And there I was, thinking you had the best possible luck in the world—"

"Sapphy always cheats," Amethyst said. If Maltravers knew her a little better, he would be able to ascertain whether she was serious or not. "Does she not, my lord?"

Maltravers swallowed. Sapphire's cousin was affixing him with a rather stern look, almost as though…

But no. Sapphire would not have told her, surely. Amethyst was still in many ways a newcomer, an outsider in the de Petras family. After her prickly beginning, her disagreements with Coral, her teasing of Micah—and that was all he knew about—he was astonished she was permitted to remain.

"—sure you could not stay another hour?" Jasper was saying from the armchair by the fire, newspaper folded in his lap. "I am more than happy to send you back in our carriage—"

"No, no, I would not dream of such a thing," Maltravers said hastily. "I am certain I will see you soon—perhaps at Lady Romeril's picnic?"

Amethyst snorted. "Do we have to attend that ridiculous—"

"You are fortunate to receive an invitation," Coral said quietly. "If you ask me."

An awkward silence descended on the drawing room, and Maltravers cleared his throat. *Most definitely time to be going.*

"I will see myself out," he said, rising from his seat and inclining his head.

His eyes came to rest on Sapphire. They had hardly had a moment to themselves all evening, their time fractured between family members eager to wish them happiness. But he had not actually spoken more than ten words together to the woman who, in the eyes of the world, would be his wife.

"Unless…" Maltravers swallowed. *What he was about to suggest was scandalous at the best of times, but…* "Unless Sapphire would be happy to accompany me to the door?"

All eyes flashed to Sapphire, who flushed. He knew what they were thinking; could see it in their glances at him, the hesitation the entire family had at approving such a plan.

They thought he wished to steal a kiss…

Trying as best he could to prevent his own face from reddening, Maltravers ensured to meet Sapphire's eyes and smile. To let her know that he had no such intentions, of course.

"Of course she will," said Jasper quietly. "Perhaps she can accompany you home."

"Jasper!"

"Sapphire cannot walk home in the dark!" protested Amethyst in astonishment.

Maltravers' heart had leapt at the man's suggestion. A few minutes with Sapphire alone would become ten, maybe even twenty. *Heavenly.*

"I do not need some sort of chaperone!" That was Sapphire, of course. "I know the streets of London well enough, and—"

"I'll send her back in my carriage," mouthed Maltravers to Jasper with a wink.

The wink was returned. "In that case, good evening, my lord."

It was a rather formal turn of phrase from the man who had taught him how to order a valet to shave oneself, thought Maltravers darkly, but there it was.

Sapphire rose. "I will not be long, Mama."

"I should think not," Opal de Petras said with a meaningful look. "Good night, James."

Maltravers nodded and left the drawing room with Sapphire just behind him.

He sighed heavily as she closed the door and they walked, slowly, toward the front door. "What was all that about?"

Sapphire rolled her eyes, and he could just make it out in the dark as his gaze became accustomed to the gloom. "I am sorry to say my Mama believes we cannot keep our hands off each other."

Maltravers almost tripped over his own feet.

"I am sorry to say that my Mama believes we cannot keep our hands off each other."

Now *that*, he could never have predicted.

"Wh-Why?" he managed, pulling on his greatcoat with relief for the excuse to look away from Sapphire for just a moment.

A moment that was all he needed. Just a moment to collect himself, to prove to himself that he could speak with a steady voice again. Not beleaguered with visions of Sapphire beneath him, naked, writhing in ecstasy—

"Well, we are engaged, aren't we?" she pointed out matter-of-factly, sadly not removing her gown but pulling on a pelisse. "They think it's a love match after your wonderful speech."

Maltravers swallowed. He had rather permitted his mouth to run away with him, which had been a mistake. The feelings he had suppressed for so long, feelings he knew would never be reciprocated, had fallen from his lips before he could stop himself.

He had made a fool of himself, yes, but only he knew just how terrible a fool.

Everyone believed those words gratefully received by the woman who now wore his ring. They could never know she had been probably laughing at him the entire time…

"Maltravers?"

He blinked. Sapphire was by the door, hand on the latch, a glove on her stub. But not her fingers.

"You aren't wearing both gloves," he said foolishly.

Sapphire flushed, eyes darting to her hand on the door. It had a rather large ring on it. "Yes. I have discovered most of my gloves do not fit this rather large bauble."

Maltravers swallowed. He should have told her, he supposed, but it had been far too easy to just give her his mother's ring and see it there, on her hand, where his heart whispered it belonged.

His stomach lurched painfully. *It would not be there forever.*

"Come on, if we don't go soon, my awful family will be assuming we are kissing like fools down here," said Sapphire with a grin, opening the door. "God's teeth, it's cold!"

Maltravers did not bother to chastise Sapphire for her curse as he followed her outside. Partly because he had never known Sapphire to pay any attention to anything anyone said if it went against her opinion in the first place, and partly because—

"Damn, it is cold," he said, laughing in surprise as Sapphire shut the front door. "And it's April!"

"Not yet summer," she said, taking a few steps along the pavement and waiting for him to join her. "Em said it was too early for warm weather, something Coral refuted but when Micah…"

Maltravers allowed her to chatter as they slowly meandered their way down the street. Oh, to be a de Petras; to truly be part of the family. The conversations they had, the laughter they shared—even the arguments would be worth having if it meant he could share in the joy.

He had wondered, when first the prickles of affection for Sapphire had started to curl their way around his heart, whether it was actually a desire to be a part of the family who had helped support him so much when his father had died, rather than a true love of the woman.

But as time had gone on, it had become clear. He liked the de Petras family, certainly, and would happily become a part of it. But he loved Sapphire.

"Maltravers?"

He blinked. "What?"

There was a teasing grin on Sapphire's face. "You haven't been listening to a word I said, have you?"

"Yes, I have," he said instinctively, then chuckled, shaking his head. "No, I haven't."

"You know, sometimes I think you've been a part of the family for years," Sapphire said wistfully. "Then I remember you have. I can't remember when you weren't, like Micah."

Maltravers' smile faltered. *Like Micah?* The last thing he wanted was to be compared to her brother!

"It is an honor to be so included by your family," he said aloud, conscious a response was necessary—even if his thoughts were not appropriate.

Sapphire, it appeared, did not agree. She rolled her eyes. "They are far too much."

"I would not say—"

"That is because you have never lived with them," she cut across him as they turned a corner. "Honestly, sometimes I think Ems was the only rational one, but even she—"

"She was the one who vowed never to marry," Maltravers pointed out with a laugh.

Goodness, to think that after all that posturing, Emerald had ended up marrying, and marrying well. Marrying a Marquess!

"—and she eloped," Sapphire was saying with a laugh. "Oh, Mal, you should have seen Mama's face when she heard the news! I thought she was going to call the nearest mail coach and abscond herself, all the way up to Scotland!"

Maltravers smiled. "I would not put that past her."

"Honestly, mothers!"

His chest tightened.

Only when he did not say anything did Sapphire glance at him, her face falling when she saw his expression. "Oh, Maltravers I—I am so sorry, I did not think—"

"I know," he said gently.

There were few people on the streets at this hour. Some like themselves returning home after a pleasant evening, others attempting to sell wares, hot pies, a last glass of ale.

"It truly does not matter—"

"Yes, it does," Sapphire said fiercely, and he heard to his surprise there was real pain in her voice. "I should not have said such a thing at all, but more so to you. I am sorry, Mal."

Hearing her pet name for him soothed any hurt he may have felt, if he could be angry at Sapphire, which Maltravers had not managed to achieve.

"They died when I was very young," he pointed out gently, drawing her arm in his as their pace slowed even further. "I hardly remember them."

"But you must miss them."

Maltravers swallowed. *Did he miss them?* It was hard to say. At least, it would have been hard to say with anyone else.

"I don't know," he said slowly. "I have no memory of my mother, but my father talked about her often. They had something rare in their station of life. A love match."

Sapphire smiled, squeezing his arm. "All my siblings have made love matches."

"And I hope one day," Maltravers found himself saying, "you will, too."

Was that a flush on her cheeks? Was it possible…no, surely not. Surely Sapphire would not have enlisted his help in this scheme—this poorly thought through scheme, though she would hear no word against it—if she had her eye on another gentleman?

Unless, and the thought gave Maltravers much pain, but he had to face it: unless this was not, in fact, a ruse to keep her family happy. Unless it was instead designed to prompt the urgings of another gentleman, a gentleman Sapphire admired but had not yet received words of adoration from?

Maltravers swallowed as he caught Sapphire's gaze and saw her smile, unpracticed and artless.

No, his Sapphire would do no such thing. It was not in her nature.

"And then your father," she said gently.

Maltravers nodded. "And then my father. A great shock, and a great absence, yes...but then, I did not know him as an adult. When I myself was grown I mean, we never conversed man to man...it is hard to know much about a person when you were so young when he died."

He swallowed. *When was the last time he had spoken about his parents?*

Now he came to think about it, did he ever speak of his parents? He could not recall doing so this year. Maybe he should. It was one way, after all, of keeping them alive.

"And that is why I cling so limpet like to your family," Maltravers said aloud, sparking a laugh from the woman beside him, which made his heart twist. "Unshifting."

"I do not quite believe my family wish you to shift, you know," Sapphire said wryly. "You are so much my brother already, we should give you the name de Petras."

Maltravers knew it was coming, knew there would be at least another comment like this through the ruse they had concocted, but that did not mean it did not hurt. And by God, it hurt.

How can you see me like that? He wanted to shout the question, demand an answer, but knew it would almost certainly pain him if he did so.

Of course she saw him as a brother. Had he ever attempted to kiss her, to woo her, to court her? Maltravers had known, the moment Emerald married and Sapphire was permitted to come out into Society, that if did not act soon...and yet he had done nothing.

Had he not chaperoned her enough times? The whole family trusted him as though he were a de Petras, or he would not have permitted to do such a thing.

"So, the question is," Maltravers said aloud, forcing his mind away from such painful thoughts as he saw they had almost reached his townhouse, "what are we going to do now?"

"Now?" Sapphire looked up, eyes wide, lips parted, and Maltravers forced himself once more not to steal a kiss from those willing lips. "What do you mean, now?"

"Now we are formally engaged," he said quietly.

"Oh." *Was that a flush of disappointment on her cheeks?*

Maltravers chastised himself silently. The more he looked for hints that were not there, the more he would drive himself utterly mad!

"Well, I must admit the whole endeavor has worked out better than I had hoped," Sapphire said, her voice strong again, as though she had recollected herself. "I never dreamed it would work so well. You know, my mother is actually asking my opinion about things now?"

Maltravers grinned. "And is she listening to your answers?"

"Not a whit, but then she never listens to my siblings," Sapphire said with a laugh, "or my father, for that matter."

"She is not a woman seeking anyone else to make the hard decisions for her," Maltravers said quietly.

It was hard not to admire a woman like that. Opal de Petras had been through much; he had been informed of a few things as a child, when his father had spoken to him of certain topics not to be discussed before the de Petras family, and he had made it his business to discover the rest when he had come of age.

The scandals that family had avoided; it was a miracle!

"No, I suppose not," said Sapphire with a smile. "Honestly, Mal, I cannot tell you how happy this has all made me."

Maltravers' heart stopped—just for a moment. His stomach was twisting painfully, his damned manhood had twitched.

Had she said—

"This false engagement has given me far more respect than I could have conceived," Sapphire continued happily. "To think, all it takes is a few pretty words and a ring, and the world considers one quite grown up."

Maltravers nodded, forcing a smile onto his face. She was happy, and her happiness gave him all the joy he needed.

Almost.

He could not pretend there was not a dark part of his heart that wished fervently she would wake up one day and see her how he saw her. As a marvel. As someone who could make the whole day brighter, just with their presence.

Oh, if she could love him, even a part of how he loved her...

But that was not the plan, Maltravers told himself firmly. And she had been quite clear about that, had she not?

There was no deception in Sapphire, it was not her nature. Not her way.

"I think it a good idea to encourage a long engagement," he said, throat dry. "The longer you can reap the benefits of your scheme, the better, I am sure."

"Oh, yes, Mama wanted to rush the whole thing and get us married in May, can you imagine!" Sapphire laughed into the stillness of the night as Maltravers worked hard not to imagine. "No, I told her autumn at the earliest, winter is best."

"You mean an engagement of a twelvemonth?" he said dryly.

There was a sparkle of mischief in her eyes as she nodded. "Of course, at the very earliest. Besides, we need to think of our escape plan."

"I don't want to escape from you."

The words had slipped from his tongue before Maltravers could halt them, but it did not appear to matter. She gave them little thought, save throwing back her head and laughing.

"Yes, I am sure you would like nothing better than to end up seeing me walk down the aisle to you, dressed in my finest gown!" Sapphire giggled.

Maltravers smiled weakly.

He had only had that dream once. Fine, a few times. She did not have to know.

"Besides, beyond extricating ourselves from my brilliant idea, we will have to think of something else of just as much import."

Maltravers glanced at Sapphire, who was smiling mischievously, and wondered what she would say if he finally declared himself. Would she think it a jest, would she understand that his words of love spoken at the Penshaw Ball were nothing less than the truth?

"Oh really?" he said, as calmly as he could manage. "And what is that?"

Sapphire winked. "We'll need time to find real spouses! You didn't think I would prevent you from finding your own countess, did you?"

Her laughter sank like knives into Maltravers' very soul. "No. No, of course not."

CHAPTER NINE

April 6, 1816

THE PARLOR WAS unusually quiet.

If Sapphire was in a teasing sort of mood, she would have said it was because she herself was being remarkably quiet. The book she had borrowed…well, stolen from Coral the last time she had visited Glaenarm House was remarkably engaging, and most of the morning had been spent ignoring her mother's invitation to go calling.

A sparkle. A glimmer, something out of the corner of her eye moved.

Sapphire very slowly twisted her left hand around the volume to see the large sapphire ring on her finger. It had been the sunlight, dancing through the stone, throwing off delightful little rays of glory. She very slightly moved her hand back and forth, making the sunlight shimmer through the ring.

It was beautiful. With each passing day that she wore it, Sapphire started to wonder where on earth he had managed to find such a thing.

Maltravers was wealthy, she knew, but earls did not spend good money on fripperies for a scheme of a friend! Surely he would not have been so ridiculous as to purposefully buy a ring from a jewelers for such an occasion?

Sapphire swallowed. She would have to ask him. Though she was remarkably careful with it, she was starting to worry it would slip off somewhere, and she would have to explain to a rather irate man who had presumably borrowed it from a fine jeweler that she had lost it.

And that would never do. The aim was to create a joyful scandal, not absolute disaster!

"Ah, there you are, Papa."

Sapphire looked up over her ring and book to see Emerald standing in the doorway, her daughter Beryl holding her hand.

Their father looked up. "Em—and Beryl and Topaz, what a delightful surprise!"

The little girl rushed toward her grandfather, leaping into his arms, and Sapphire smiled. It was always wonderful to have her nieces come to visit.

"Ah, I see I am intruding."

Sapphire dropped her book, but thankfully the beautiful ring stayed on her finger as Maltravers grinned from the door.

"Not expecting me?"

"Always expecting you," quipped Sapphire, grateful her voice was stronger than her nerves. *What on earth had made her so startled to see the man she cared for?* "You almost live here, Mal, you should move into Micah's old room."

"Never fear," said Maltravers as he stepped into the room and bowed to Jasper, before settling on the sofa beside her. "If I lived here, I'd have to put up with your nonsense even more so than I do now."

Sapphire punched him lightly and smiled.

Why was it that everything felt so much more…more right, whenever Maltravers was in the room? Even here, in the parlor, which by all rights should be entirely restricted to family and family alone, the place seemed complete with Maltravers.

A lack of him, Sapphire was starting to see, was not compatible with her happiness.

"It's wonderful to see you," she said impulsively.

For some reason, her statement caused a little color to rush into his cheeks. Sapphire stared. When was the last time she had seen her friend…well, flush was the only word she could think of to describe whatever this was supposed to be.

What had she said?

"Your nieces look happy," he said quietly.

Sapphire glanced across the room and grinned as Beryl and Topaz sat in her grandfather's lap, the elder entertaining him with a long story that appeared to be about a stick. She was almost a little too big for his lap now, but she curled up into him just as she had done for years.

"She is always happy when she's here," Sapphire said with a smile. "They all are. It's a de Petras thing, I think."

"I understand it well," came the quiet reply.

She shot a look at him. There was something…different about Maltravers. Something she had not noticed when he had first entered the room, and even now she had registered it was there, she could not put her finger precisely on what was different.

But it was different.

His clothing was the same. The same old jacket she knew so well, that darn mark in the elbow that you could only see if you were really looking. His valet really was a marvel.

Was it when they had gone riding and Maltravers had got caught on a bramble, or when they had gone to the cattle market—something her mother had certainly not approved of— and caught himself on a splinter in the fence? Either way, there it was.

The cravat might be new—

"Why are you staring at me, Sapphy?"

Sapphire grinned, heat searing her own cheeks. "I just—there is something different about you, Mal, and I am attempting to figure it out."

He laughed quietly as Emerald murmured with her daughters. "You've only just noticed?"

Now this was a challenge. Sapphire sat up straighter and pushed her book more firmly onto the console table beside her, focusing all her attention on the gentleman beside her.

"You mean to tell me it's something I should have noticed before?"

His dark eyes met hers, and there was something different about them, too. More stormy. Bolder, somehow, though that was not quite right, even Sapphire had to admit that.

"Oh, yes," Maltravers said lightly, a grin teasing on his lips. "It's something I thought you would have remarked on by now, but of course if you have not noticed it…"

"I will," said Sapphire fiercely. *She was not about to be outdone.* "Here, look at me a moment."

His eyes did not waver from hers, and for some inexplicable reason, something rather odd happened.

Sapphire…leaned.

It was only to get a better view of the man, she told herself firmly. After all, if it was something she had missed these last weeks—odd, because they had spent more time together than ever, now that their pretend engagement was out in the open, and they had hardly spent little time together before.

Something different.

Her gaze raked over him. There was the same old jaw line, crisp and elegantly shaved. His hair was the same, though a little ruffled. His jacket was the same, most definitely…

"Are you…wearing a different style cravat?" Sapphire hazarded.

She flushed as Maltravers laughed. "You're looking in the wrong place, Sapph."

"Well, it is not as though you are giving me much of a clue!" she retorted hotly.

"It would not be very impressive if I had to help you," he pointed out, lowering his voice so her family did not hear him. "Come on, Sapphire. I thought…well. I thought you were pretending not to notice."

Pretending not to notice? Sapphire swallowed and focused once more on the gentleman sitting beside her. It was most irritating. She would work it out. Who knew him better, after all?

But as her gaze moved to his chest, the gold buttons the same, the pocket watch chain the same—that would never alter, it had been his father's, from memory—Sapphire had to admit, if only to herself, that she could not see a spot different.

Even his boots were the same.

Sapphire looked back up at Maltravers' face, about to admit, most reluctantly, that she after all need an additional clue.

But her voice caught in her throat. Maltravers was looking at her.

No, that did not do him justice; he was not merely looking at her, but examining her, staring, an intensity in his eyes that she had never seen before. She had been right at the beginning, her instincts leading her true.

There was something in the eyes, something stormy, something…Sapphire would have called it passionate if that expression had been in the eyes of anyone else.

But in Maltravers…

Something strange shivered down her spine. *What was going on?*

"Sapphire," Maltravers breathed, "I—"

"There you are!"

Sapphire started. Somehow, she had managed to find herself mere inches away from Maltravers, of all people, and only the sudden arrival of her brother had made her notice it.

Which was most irregular. She had no need, and certainly no desire to be close to Maltravers. It did not explain why her fingers were tingling, or her heart racing in a most strange way.

She cleared her throat. "Here we are."

Why was her voice so weak?

"You were looking for us, Micah?" Jasper said calmly from the other side of the room.

Sapphire dropped her gaze to her hand and stub in her lap as she smoothed her skirts, trying to keep her heart calm, though that did not seem to make any difference.

What had happened in that moment? Maltravers had not done anything, he could not be blamed for how she was feeling…

If she even understood how she was feeling. It was most distressing, in a way, thinking about how every part of her had been…well, quivering was not the right word, but—

"I've just come from Coral's, Mama is there," said Micah in a rush. "It's Catherine."

Sapphire's stomach dropped into her feet, mouth falling open as she stared at Micah.

His face was flushed. Was that because he had run all the way from Glaenarm House—unlikely—or worse, because something had happened. Something dreadful.

Beryl slipped to the floor as Jasper rose urgently. "Catherine, she—"

"She's fine," said Micah, still panting as he leaned against the wall of the parlor. He ran a hand through his hair.

Sapphire's throat seemed to be closing, panic rushing through her—or was it dread? She could hardly tell. Why wasn't Micah saying anything? Why had he rushed here like a wild thing if Catherine was…

Oh, but of course. Oh, Lord, if Catherine was fine, and Micah was evidently fine, other than looking terribly out of breath, which could only mean—

"And the child—the baby?" Emerald said in a whisper as she pulled Beryl and Topaz closer to her. "It is fine, too?"

Micah shook his head. "No."

Sapphire swallowed the cry she had been about to let out. She would not permit herself to cry here, not before the family—though strangely, Maltravers' presence did not matter. She could cry in front of him, had done before. At least twice, now she came to think about it.

It was dangerous, wasn't it, having a child? Her mother had always said that, said every mother took their lives into their hands when it was time for their child to come.

But she had been safe, and both her sisters had children with little complication whatsoever. Dr Walsingham had attended, naturally, but he had not had to do anything.

But Catherine—

"It's not fine," said Micah steadily, eyes dancing, "because there are two of them."

Sapphire blinked. She could not have heard that correctly. *Two of them?*

"Two—two of them?" she spluttered, rising to her feet. "Micah de Petras!"

Without waiting for him to say anything, she strode across the room and not so gently punched him in the arm.

"Sapphy!"

"Sapphire de Petras!"

"Ouch, Sapphy, that hurt!"

"Good," said Sapphire darkly as she embraced her fool of a brother. "Because you near on gave me a heart attack, you fool!"

Jagged laughter escaped from her lungs as she clutched the man who had just, it appeared, become a father. The whole room seemed to relax as Micah embraced her in turn.

"Never," said their father as he approached, a fierce look on his face as Sapphire released Micah, "do that to me again."

Sapphire smiled as Jasper pulled Micah into an embrace of his own.

"I promise," said Micah with a laugh. "At least, Catherine has informed me we will never be having any more children, so I doubt I will have the opportunity!"

Maltravers slapped the man on the arm, and Sapphire jumped. She had not noticed him leave the sofa, and he was remarkably close to her. Very close. Why was she suddenly so conscious of how close Mal was?

"And both babes, they are well? Healthy?"

"Healthy and screaming," Micah answered Emerald with a wild laugh. "I do not think I will ever know peace again."

"Good," said Sapphire, laughing in turn. "It was time you halted your wild life!"

The whole place was filled with laughter now, and Sapphire stepped back so Emerald could congratulate their brother. It was strange, she had known Micah and Catherine's babe—or babies, of course—would be arriving soon, but to have them here, it made the whole thing so real, somehow.

He was gone.

Sapphire was not sure how she knew, but Maltravers' lack of presence suddenly rushed into her consciousness. She turned in search of him and smiled, shoulders relaxing from the tension she had not even known was there, as she saw him standing a little way away, on the other side of the room.

"Twins," she said with a smile as she wandered over to him.

Maltravers nodded. "Your brother is going to have his hands full."

"Good," said Sapphire, grinning. "He's one that could do with being kept in line."

"He's a fortunate man," said Maltravers softly. There was something strange in his expression again, and Sapphire stepped closer, as though that would help her ascertain precisely what it was. "A man who knew what he wanted and took it."

Sapphire stared. This was not the Maltravers she knew; a man who spoke in riddles, who did not look at her as he always had done, but instead looked at her like…like…

She swallowed. If she did not know any better, and she did, she would say something had changed between them—and the very thought caused a spark of panic to rush through her whole body.

Changed? The idea of not having Maltravers, of losing him, was unthinkable. A dagger of ice sliced into her heart and forced her lips to part in shock.

What if…and she had thought about this flippantly once or twice but never given it much heed, but she could not ignore it now. What if Maltravers really did find someone else?

Not another friend, but a woman he wished to marry?

Unconsciously, Sapphire broke the connection of their gazes to look at her ring.

A sapphire. A sapphire for Sapphire, her brother had quipped when she had first shown him the ring, and she had laughed then, thought Maltravers clever to have thought of it.

But one day he would take this back from her, would he not, and give it to another? Another woman. Someone else who would laugh at his jokes and go walking with him, help her cheat at cards and gossip with her about all the great and the good in London.

Sapphire raised her eyes and met Maltravers' gaze. There was something powerful there, something she did not understand, but part of her did. A part of her that she did not appear to be able to reach, though it was there.

"Maltravers—"

"Sapphire, come and listen to this!"

Sapphire swallowed. "Say something," she whispered, eyes unmoving.

But Maltravers merely smiled, and breathed, "What would you have me say?"

"Sapphy!"

"What?" snapped Sapphire, turning most unwillingly away from the man who had always been so understandable and was now completely incomprehensible.

It was Emerald who had spoken. It was most unlike her to demand anyone's attention.

"Come and listen to this," her sister repeated with a small laugh. "Your brother has something to tell you."

Sapphire did not stomp, precisely, but her temper was rather frayed as she obeyed her older sister and crossed the room.

Surely Maltravers was about to admit what it was, whatever it was, that had changed within him. Had the change been recent? Was it of great duration, and she had merely missed it?

But she spent almost all her time with Maltravers; how could she have missed something so important?

Micah was smiling ruefully, Beryl now in his arms as though she had demanded a little attention after such a fuss had been made for her uncle, and for no good reason.

"Tell her," prompted Emerald, eyes sparkling.

Sapphire looked between her sister and brother. "Tell me what?"

Micah sighed and rolled his eyes. "Emerald was asking about my children."

"And?" Sapphire had not intended to snap, and thankfully her siblings appeared to be too euphoric from the news to really notice.

It was maddening. At any other time, Micah's news—Micah and Catherine's news, really—would have taken all her attention, and quite rightly so.

But Sapphire could not help but feel the back of her neck prickle as Maltravers' gaze surely looked across the room at her. She had never been so conscious of the man before.

What was going on?

"They are both girls, of course," said Micah with a laugh. "There was never any possibility, I suppose, that there would be another boy in the family!"

Sapphire managed to laugh with Emerald; it was clearly what was expected, so she joined in. But her heart was not in it. How could it be? Of course they were girls, now she came to think about it, she could not have expected it to be anything else.

It was not her two new nieces that were absorbing all her attention, or the one who was here, tugging on her gown; it was the gentleman behind them all who was whirling through her mind.

She knew Maltravers, knew him better than anyone. So why was he able to be so mystifying now?

A scream.

Sapphire whirled around, Emerald beside her doing the same thing but a fraction faster. Perhaps it was something about being a mother.

Topaz had tripped and fallen—at least, almost fallen. Her scream had been instinctual, it appeared, at the very act of falling, but she had not bruised herself nor bumped her head for hands swift and steady had caught her, bringing her into his arms.

Maltravers' arms.

Sapphire swallowed. As Emerald rushed forward to take her daughter into her arms, Sapphire just stared.

Maltravers, standing there with a child in his arms who looked remarkably like herself…like a child of theirs would look.

She pushed the thought away hurriedly. *What nonsense!* It was ridiculous to even consider such a thing—scandalous, too, really, for no lady should be so presumptuous about a gentleman, even in the privacy of her own thoughts.

And this was Maltravers! Not just any old gentleman, but her…her friend.

"Oh, thank you, Maltravers, I am so grateful—"

"Not at all, I'm merely glad to be of service," came his smiling reply.

Sapphire swallowed. This was all rather odd. When she had concocted this little scheme, this ruse of an engagement—which she was still certain was a brilliant idea, and no one could convince her out of that…

Well. She had not expected this. Whatever this was.

CHAPTER TEN

April 8, 1816

"REMIND ME," SAID Maltravers darkly, "why are we doing this again?"

His cravat was most uncomfortable. The moment his valet had heard about this evening's invitation, of course, the blasted man had insisted on attempting something different, and it was most irritating.

Maltravers tugged at the closely woven cravat but could find no relief. His companion laughed.

"It is no laughing matter, Sapphire," he said tartly as they stepped up the marble steps into the large townhouse. "May I remind you that this is going to be very…public."

He had to force himself to keep his voice calm as he spoke.

Oh, if only he had been bold enough, brave enough to say something a few days ago when he and Sapphire…

It had not been a moment. Had it? Maltravers could hardly tell, his heart had been racing so rapidly at the time he was rather impressed he had managed to stay conscious.

"Say something."

"What would you have me say?"

He swallowed as a footman removed his greatcoat and another took Sapphire's pelisse. He had no idea what had got into him that day. It was all this pretending to be engaged, that's what it was. A man could only bear so much.

And so he had tried to tell her, in his own way, just how much he cared. Had she understood?

"Are you…wearing a different style cravat?"

"You're looking in the wrong place, Sapph."

"Well, it is not as though you are giving me much of a clue!"

"It would not be very impressive if I had to help you. Come on, Sapphire. I thought…well. I thought you were pretending not to notice."

Maltravers sighed heavily. No, she had not, and worst of all, he had not had the gumption to do anything about it. There she had been, all delightful and beautiful as she always was, which was probably now he came to think about it why he had been unable to say the precise words…

Sapphire, I love you.

"Sapphire!"

Maltravers jumped, but it was only Coral, advancing up the same steps wearing the most outlandish mixture of feathers and ribbons in her hair he had ever seen.

"Lord, Coral, did a peacock fly into your hair?" said Sapphire with a laugh.

Maltravers did his best to keep his face calm as he watched the two sisters bicker.

"—know full well it is the fashion, how dare you cast aspersions on my maid—"

"It's not your maid I'm worried about, it's the peacock! What if it comes alive again?"

Mischief danced across the face of the woman he loved, and Maltravers did what he could to stay out of the warpath of the oldest de Petras sibling as she strode past, nose in the air.

Her husband, Edward, shot them both a grin. "You've done it now, Sapphire."

"Oh, Coral will overcome my petty remarks, I am sure," said Sapphire with a giggle. "On you go, you had better rescue whoever she has accosted next—if that peacock hasn't first!"

"Sapphire!" her brother-in-law said warningly, though it was mired a little by the grin he gave her, and then he, too, entered the corridor.

Sapphire sighed heavily. "Goodness, she is remarkably easy to tease."

"As are you," Maltravers pointed out as they stood in the hallway.

It could not just be him who was unwilling to go forward, was it? Why did she not suggest they enter?

"Yes, I suppose you are right," said Sapphire airily. "I mean, this entire scheme was concocted merely because I did not wish people to tease me. Blast you, Mal, do you always have to be right?"

Maltravers permitted himself a grin. "Yes."

She laughed, tapping him on the arm. "I'll remember that."

He had stiffened the moment she approached him. It was most unfair that he was barely able to control himself when the woman was near him, but then, as Maltravers reminded himself, it had been that way for years and she had not noticed.

Why, even when he had attempted to draw attention to himself and show her, somehow, with his eyes just how he felt about her—though admittedly it would have been a lot clearer if he had just used his damn tongue…

Perhaps he should have kissed her. *Perhaps*, thought Maltravers wildly, *he should now.*

Desire was rushing through him, easily able to overwhelm his good manners and senses. There was no one else here, after all, they were quite alone and—

"Ah, the Penshaws," said Sapphire.

Maltravers took a hasty step back. Not that he was too close to her—in his view, not damned close enough—but probably a little too close for comfort.

"Oh, just the sister," she added, looking curiously at the lady who entered on the arm of a gentleman Maltravers did not recognize. "You know, I have not seen the duke this entire

Season, have you?"

"What?" said Maltravers blankly.

Well, how was he supposed to focus with Sapphire looking all...all like that?

"You are frowning."

"No, I'm not," he said hastily. *Blast.* How did she do that? Always know precisely when he wished to have no attention on him, when he wished to...to look at her. "You were saying. Before Coral got here."

Sapphire blinked as they stepped aside for Lady Margaret to have her pelisse removed by a footman. "I was?"

Maltravers smiled gently. "About why we are doing this. Of all places we could have come tonight—"

"Oh, are you drowning in invitations?" Sapphire teased him, an eyebrow raised.

He had to laugh. "A little! You try being the Earl of Maltravers, you'll find yourself inundated with invitations from people you barely know to events you have no wish to attend!"

"You know, I may well do just that," said Sapphire, tapping him on the arm.

Maltravers swallowed. He could feel the place where Sapphire had touched him like a burn, like a brand, marking him for herself. Could she feel it? Was that why her eyes had become unfocused for a moment, as though the whole world had rushed around her before settling?

"Well, you are about to become Lady Maltravers, I suppose," he said quietly.

He should not have said it. It was a dream, that was all; this ruse was not reality, and he had to stop himself from thinking as though it was. As though Sapphire had agreed to marry him for his own sake, and not the way it could tease her family. As though his mother's ring on her finger was there to stay...

Sapphire snorted. "I suppose I am. Well, we are here because Lady Romeril is one of my mother's closest friends."

Without a second thought, she slipped her hand through

Maltravers' arm and started to direct him along toward the corridor that would lead to the ballroom.

"Your mother's closest friend?"

She nodded as they walked slowly along the corridor, brilliantly lit with countless candles. "Yes. She did a service for my mother once, years ago, before I was born—"

"BC," said Maltravers with a laugh. "Before Chaos."

He was rewarded, as he knew he would be, with a gentle punch on the arm. Oh, how he wished she would touch him more; teasing her was the only way he could wangle it, a most scandalous strategy.

If she had any idea he quizzed her so on purpose, merely to get the slightest touch…

"Lady Romeril and my mother are dear friends, Mal," said Sapphire severely as she inclined her head to a guest, "so I hope you will be on your best behavior."

"Maybe," he said dryly. "But that does not explain why she is hosting a ball for us."

It was a concern brewing in his chest ever since the invitation had arrived.

Lady Romeril requires your attendance at a ball in your honor, April 8, at 8pm sharp.

"She did not even request an RSVP," pointed out Maltravers, his stomach churning. "There goes a woman who is absolutely certain she will get what she wants."

"She usually does," said Sapphire with a laugh. "Something to aim for, I'd say."

"Like you never get what you want."

"You're right, everyone should bow to me and hand over gifts when I pass," she said, giggling again. "No, in all seriousness, as my godmother—"

"Your godmother?"

Maltravers worked hard to prevent his face from falling. There were few people who could truly make or break a reputation in Society; most of those who believed they had that power were merely hoping it would one day become so.

But not Lady Romeril.

She was a stalwart of good Society, in it so long she almost had the power to dictate who was impressive and who should be avoided. Her authority was not absolute, of course, but it was impressive. To make an enemy of Lady Romeril was to be very foolish indeed.

And now the woman was hosting his engagement ball? What would happen when she discovered, as she surely would eventually, that the engagement was not going to lead to a wedding?

Worse, what if she discovered it had never intended to in the first place?

"—nice thing for me, as her goddaughter," Sapphire was saying, then dropped her voice as they reached the double doors to the ballroom, "though if you ask me, it is more because it does not appear Lady Rose will marry. Lady Romeril will have little opportunity to celebrate without making a great fuss over me."

Maltravers' stomach churned. "Great fuss?"

Sapphire smiled as they halted just outside the double doors. There was such certainty in her smile, such power that flowed through her that for a moment, he almost forgot this whole thing was a pretense.

Here they were, arm in arm, at their own engagement ball. Him and Sapphire. Just as he had always hoped.

"Great fuss indeed," said Sapphire, arching an eyebrow. "I presumed it is quite alright with you, Mal? You agreed to this, you know. The sham. Do not tell me, on the eve of our engagement ball, that you wish to have your ring back?"

Maltravers could not help himself. He glanced at the hand in his arm, his mother's jewel sparkling there on the finger of the woman he adored with all his heart.

Have the ring back? If he had his way, it would never leave her finger.

Not that he could admit to that.

Besides, she was right. Lady Romeril was about to make a great fuss of them, and he could almost feel the excitement radiating from Sapphire's body. She, the youngest, the one who never had much of a fuss made of her at all—Micah was already getting into too much trouble by the time she reached an age to be noticed—was finally about to have her moment.

Was he truly suggesting to take it away, merely because he was piqued she did not love him—did not return an affection he had been too cowardly to declare?

"Mal?"

Maltravers forced a smile. "I…well, I am a little afraid of Lady Romeril."

Sapphire giggled.

Sound was starting to drift underneath the doors behind them; music, chatter, laughter. It appeared most of Society had been invited by Lady Romeril to their engagement ball, and that would mean a great many eyes on them, of course.

"She is nothing to be afraid of."

"Of course, you're not afraid of her," said Maltravers dryly. "You grew up with her."

There was a rather knowing smile on her face, which made her eyes sparkle all the more. "I grew up with you, too."

A weak smile crept across his lips, and he wished desperately he had the bravery to just lean and kiss those passionate lips. Show her, not tell her, what she meant to him. Make Sapphire see that he could make her happy, happier than she had ever been.

"You know, sometimes I think you've been a part of the family for years. Then I remember you have. I can't remember when you weren't, like Micah."

His smile faded. But of course, she would not wish that, nor welcome it. He was not the sort of cad to demand a kiss from an unwilling partner.

"Well," he said quietly, "here we go."

Forcing a smile on his face that felt a little brittle, Maltravers reached out and opened the first of the double doors. The other opened swiftly after, moved by a footman standing on the other side of the door.

A wave of sound hit them as he and Sapphire stepped forward.

"James Gresley, the Earl of Maltravers and his betrothed, Miss Sapphire de Petras, goddaughter of our gracious hostess," announced a man in Romeril livery, bellowing the words over the genteel applause now echoing around the room.

Maltravers did his best to keep his smile intact, but the moment he glanced at Sapphire, it broadened into a natural grin.

She looked so happy. Radiant, her smile so natural and excited that there was nothing he could do but glory in her. Sapphire de Petras. Any man would be fortunate to have her on his arm, and it was his honor.

"Such a wonderful couple," he heard someone say as they stepped forward into the ballroom, nodding at those who called out well wishes.

"—did not expect such an announcement, I must say," said someone else.

"—even more advancement for the de Petras—"

"—a countess, the wedding should be spectacular—"

Maltravers swallowed as Sapphire's hand tightened on his arm.

"Isn't it wonderful?" she breathed with shining eyes.

He nodded, rather than risk saying anything. Oh, it was wonderful at the moment, yes; but it would all change one day, and then what?

The scandal of their broken engagement would, he was sure, make Sapphire a delicate proposition for anyone creating an invitation list to dinners, card parties, balls, and the like. Would she be ostracized, ignored by Society? Would it be presumed there was something amiss with her?

They really did need to think of a plan, Maltravers thought darkly as they reached the other side of the room and halted, turning to smile at Lady Romeril's guests.

Another squeeze on his arm. Maltravers looked at Sapphire to see her positively glowing with pleasure.

"I did not expect this," she murmured, eyes bright. "So many people!"

"So many people care about you," Maltravers found himself saying. "They want what is best for you. As…as do I."

The words had slipped from his lips before he could stop them, but Sapphire grinned.

"Of course you do," she said lightly.

Maltravers' stomach twisted, but he could say no more. One day, yes, one day he would admit his feelings to Sapphire…but this was not the right time.

"So, you decided hosting your own engagement party would be insufficient."

Maltravers felt the change in Sapphire. Her grip tightened on his arm, her whole body went rigid, then slackened as he watched her smile at a woman who approached her.

"Antoinette," he heard Sapphire say boldly. "I did not think you would be so openly bitter about my engagement."

"Bitter? Moi?" The woman Sapphire called Antoinette laughed. "I would not say an engagement of this sort was one to celebrate, would you? A rather convenient engagement, is it not?"

Maltravers' heart skipped a beat. *It was impossible—how could she possibly know?*

It did not appear likely that Sapphire would have confided her plan into a woman like this, standing there and smiling happily at the evident discomfort she had caused. So how on earth did she know?

"I do not know what you are talking about," Sapphire said imperiously.

He almost applauded, right there and then. How did she do it? How did Sapphire know precisely what to say?

"Well, it is a pity engagement, is it not?" Antoinette leaned forward and smiled cattily. "His lordship felt sorry for you, did he not? All your siblings married, no wonder your friend the earl wished to put you out of your misery and—"

"And where is your husband, Mrs…?" Maltravers interrupted darkly.

She was fortunate she was a lady, he thought bitterly, for if she had been a man and speaking like that to Sapphire, he would have forced the brute out of the place, whether it was his ball or not.

The cheek!

"M-My husband?" Antoinette looked disconcerted. "I am not—"

"In that case, I do not think you are the one to be casting judgment, do you?" said Maltravers, raising an eyebrow. "Come on, Sapphire. Let us go and converse with those worth our time."

Sapphire breathed out slowly as they stepped across the ballroom. "I am sorry about that."

Maltravers' stomach clenched. *That she thought she had to apologize to him!* "There is nothing to apologize for."

"I mean, really, saying you would wish to marry me just for pity!" she said under her breath with brittleness in her tone. "As if you would wish to marry me at all!"

This was his chance, Maltravers knew; he could say something, anything to give Sapphire a hint that actually, that was precisely what he wished to do, immediately.

"Now, will you dance with me?"

Maltravers blinked. Sapphire had released his arm and had a mischievous smile. "I beg your pardon?"

"Well, this is a ball, isn't it?" she pointed out as musicians started up a tune, and couples started to move forward to make up a set. "And I thought, as I essentially asked you to marry me, I may as well ask you to dance, too."

Maltravers smiled weakly. *How was he ever to explain to this woman what he felt?*

"Come on," said Sapphire impetuously, taking him by the hand.

Would he ever be able to say no to her? He doubted it; not

that he had ever wanted to, which was perhaps what made it so difficult now.

But as Maltravers stood opposite Sapphire in the set, waiting for the musical note that would begin the dance, he took all of her in. The beauty, the elegance, the fiery spirit that had made him fall in love with her. None of that would change. Oh, her looks would change, probably, as would his. The real Sapphire, the intelligent remarks and joy, that would remain.

Sapphire curtseyed, and Maltravers bowed, then stepped forward with all the gentlemen and took her hand and stub in his hands.

It was astonishing.

They had danced together before; he could recall helping to teach Sapphire some of the more complex dances when they had both been younger.

But this was different. A fiery heat flooded through Maltravers' body—and if he was not mistaken, hers, too.

Somehow, and he did not understand how, he had finally had an effect on her. Or was he dreaming it? Was it possible that he was able to fool himself?

But no—as Sapphire turned and Maltravers, as the dance dictated, placed his hands on her waist, he could feel a quivering excitement rushing through her that had never been there before.

He tried not to gently stroke the material of her gown at her waist, refusing all temptation to pull her tighter, but as though she could somehow hear his thoughts, Sapphire shifted as they promenaded down the set, leaning closer to him.

He breathed in the heady scent of Sapphire, a medley of lavender and something else he had never managed to guess, and tried desperately to think.

He had to dance. He had to keep himself controlled, he had to—

"Come with me."

Sapphire's words had been breathed, no one else could possibly hear them, but Maltravers did not stop to think. He obeyed, sure he would do anything if Sapphire requested it. Anything she wanted.

Her hand slipped in his, pulling him away from the dancers—attracting a number of astonished looks, from what Maltravers could see—out of the double doors, along the corridor they had so recently walked down, then into a room on the left.

Maltravers had so rarely come to this part of the Romeril house that for a moment he did not know where he was. Then he saw, in the dark of the evening, a drawing room, a low blaze in the grate.

A door slammed. Maltravers started and turned to see Sapphire, who must have slipped through his fingers, leaning against the door.

"What," she said in an undertone, her eyes fixed on his as she stepped toward him, "was that?"

Maltravers swallowed. He was reading too much into this, surely. It could not, she could not mean what he thought she did. "I don't know what you—"

"Yes you do," said Sapphire, standing mere inches before him, her bold gaze not leaving his own. "You know exactly what I mean, Mal."

Maltravers tried to breathe, tried to think, tried to tell himself that what he wanted to do in that moment would be madness—

He kissed her.

It was very sudden, a quick lean forward and the kiss he had dreamt of for years was taken. A gentle brush across her lips, he had no wish to take liberties—no, that was not quite true, he wanted to pull her to the floor and make love to her.

Maltravers swallowed. Sapphire was looking up at him, eyes flushed, lips parted, eyes wide.

But she had not gone. He had to hold onto that, did he not? She had not—

"I don't understand," Sapphire breathed, and there was an ache in her voice he had never heard before.

And she stepped forward, raised her hand and placed it on her chest. She could surely feel now, if she had not been able to hear before, his frantically beating heart. Maltravers knew it was over, this whole ruse, their friendship perhaps, for he had kissed her, kissed Sapphire—

But perhaps not. She had not slapped him for taking such a liberty, not chastised him for it.

Maltravers hesitated. *So did that mean…*

"I don't understand either," he breathed, utterly at a loss.

He watched her swallow, watched her hesitate. "Why did you—"

"I don't know," he said hurriedly. At least that was the truth. What had come over him, that he would break his self-control like that?

Sapphire nodded as she offered up her lips. "Then…then I think you should do it again."

He must have misheard. "I beg your par—"

"So that we can understand," said Sapphire quietly, eyes never leaving his. "I want to understand, Mal. We are friends, we both know it—it means nothing. So kiss me."

He groaned as he pulled his arms around the woman he loved and lowered his lips onto hers, powerfully this time, boldly, with all the passion he had been restraining for so long.

And she responded. Sapphire, his Sapphire, moaned at the pleasure he hoped he was giving her, but then if she was not enjoying his kisses then why were her lips parting, why were her hands around his neck, why was she pressing herself into him as though she never wished to be parted?

How long they were kissing, Maltravers was not sure.

Eventually, however, he broke the kiss and halted, breathing heavy, heart pounding, and stomach churning. He had just had the most incredible kiss of his life.

"W-Well?" he said quietly, hating the nerves in his voice.

Sapphire smiled gently. "I think further study is required."

CHAPTER ELEVEN

April 11, 1814

"MAMA," SAID SAPPHIRE quietly. "I…I have a favor to ask."
Opal de Petras looked up from the papers she was reading on the sofa in the parlor. She had been there sometime; Sapphire had been watching her.

Waiting.

Waiting for the right moment to speak. Eventually her impatience had got the better of her, as she had expected. But really, what on earth could her mother be reading that was that interesting, and that long?

It was maddening.

"A favor?" Opal smiled. "You are not usually one to ask for favors, Sapphire."

"So I needed someone I could trust. Call it…call it a favor after a lifetime of friendship."

Sapphire felt her cheeks flush, knew they were red, boiling red if the sensation was anything to go by, and wished to goodness she had better control of herself.

But how could she, with her mother reminding her of the favor she so recently asked Maltravers? A favor which had felt easy, straightforward, when she had first asked. How difficult would it be for her friend to pretend to be her betrothed for a few months?

It felt anything but easy now.

"W-Well?"

"I think further study is required."

Sapphire swallowed. She had done her best to put that evening out of her mind. Her best was not particularly good, the memories of Maltravers kissing her most ardently intruding in her thoughts almost every minute of the day…

But still. She was trying.

It was ridiculous, she told herself silently as she smiled at her mother and attempted to think about how she could ask this question.

Maltravers and her, kissing!

It was ludicrous. If anyone had told her that she would be kissing Maltravers most passionately in one of Lady Romeril's drawing rooms, she would have laughed in their face.

It would never happen!

Yet it had. And after that first kiss, light on her lips yet making her heart soar, Sapphire had done what she could never have predicted. She had asked—ordered, really—a gentleman to kiss her.

That was all very well…but it was Maltravers. Maltravers!

"I think further study is required."

And she would not have had to ask him to kiss her again if he had not been so—so infuriatingly warm. So irritatingly close, so present, so strong as he had held her—

"Sapphire?"

Sapphire blinked. How long had she got lost in her thoughts of Maltravers' kiss this time? She was starting to get a reputation in her family for daydreaming.

Little could they guess that she was not imagining some fanciful thoughts, merely reliving a fantastical moment. Which was why she had decided to ask her mother a favor.

It had been three days.

"I wondered, Mama," Sapphire said aloud, wishing her voice

was calmer and wondering if her mother had noticed, "if you would invite Maltravers to dinner this evening?"

She had expected questions; expected her mother to frown, to wonder why, to say that she could not simply change that evening's preparations, that Cook would be most put out at changing things with such little notice.

But true to form, Opal did nothing that was expected of her.

"Of course," she said lightly, turning from daughter to papers. "Send a note."

Sapphire stared. "What?"

Her mother looked up. "Did I stutter?"

"No, but—"

"I said yes, Sapphire, so send that note, or even better, go around yourself," said Opal with a grin. "You thought I would say no?"

"I…" Sapphire hesitated. She was not entirely sure what she had expected, now she came to think about it.

That was the trouble, wasn't it? Now Maltravers was her betrothed—and sometimes she had to remind herself that, lost as she was in the memories of his scalding kisses—everyone assumed she wished to spend every waking moment with him.

And the thing was…she did.

"Yes, it's always pleasant to have James here."

"James?"

Opal frowned. "James, Sapphire. James Gresley, the Earl of Maltravers—your betrothed? What has got into you today?"

"Oh. Oh, of course," Sapphire said weakly.

It was strange to think of Maltravers as anything other than Maltravers—but of course, he did have a first name. And a surname. Calling him by his title was something she had got into the habit of when very young, probably because her father called him that.

Sapphire tested out his name in her mind, silently. *James.*

She almost snorted. No, that would never do.

"—one of the politest guests we ever have," her mother was

saying. "You know, in a way, he is almost our second son already. Has been for years."

A strange sort of discomfort stirred in Sapphire's stomach. *Second son?*

To be sure, she had considered Maltravers as a brother for a while now, years perhaps. She had even told him so recently, had she not? She had a vague memory of saying that, and at the time it had felt completely natural.

But now…something had changed. What it was, she did not know, but it felt wrong. Her heart rebelled, skipping a beat at the very idea.

What was going on?

"Sapphire?"

"What?" Sapphire said hastily, looking up.

Her mother was smiling. "The note."

"Note?" she repeated wildly. *What on earth was her mother talking about?*

"To James," Opal said pointedly. "Inviting him to dinner. Won't you write one?"

Sapphire smiled weakly. "Yes. Yes, I will. Thank you, Mama."

Thankfully, it was only a few hours until evening came, the nights taking longer and longer to arrive as they grew closer to summer, and Sapphire did not have to sit in the drawing room with her ears pricked for the sound of the door for long.

"There! He's here!" Sapphire said impulsively, looking at the door eagerly.

"Is he indeed?" said Jasper quietly, reading his newspaper by the fire.

How could he sit so still? Sapphire could feel every inch of her body quivering at the idea of Maltravers walking into this room. To think, in just a moment he would be here, his smile filling the room, that powerful presence he had taking over her senses…

The door opened.

"Good evening," said Maltravers with a broad smile.

Sapphire leaped from her seat and rushed over to him. "Maltravers!"

She had kissed him on the cheek, breathing in that heady masculine scent she had never noticed, before she knew what she was doing.

Sapphire blinked. She was close to him, too close—*yet not close enough.* Where had that thought come from? She needed to move, needed to step away, but her feet were not moving, no part of her body was obeying.

Maltravers had turned to look at her, his lips a mere inch from her own, and was that his hand on the small of her back and—

"Give the man some room, Sapphy, he'll still need to breathe!"

As though scalded, Sapphire stepped back, and Maltravers' gentle touch disappeared. An ache of disappointment curled around her heart, which made no sense.

"Come on in, James, do not let my wild daughter distract you," said Opal with a laugh.

Sapphire flushed, and saw Maltravers flush in turn with surprise. Why was he embarrassed? It had been she who had rushed toward him like a wild thing, evidently making a fool of herself.

And yet, perhaps not. Her parents believed them….in love, did they not? It was a rather unpredicted side effect of her ruse; her parents believed she loved him.

Sapphire smiled weakly. "I-I am glad you are here."

Why did her voice quiver?

"And I am glad to be here and glad you are glad," Maltravers said in a rush. The color on his cheeks darkened.

Oh, it was all too confusing—and the worst of it was, Sapphire was almost certain she knew what he was thinking, why his cheeks were so pink, as hers undoubtedly were.

He was thinking of that night… When they had been so foolish as to lose themselves in the moment.

For that was what it had to be, Sapphire told herself. They had merely got swept up in the excitement; of their plan, its success, the friendly wishes at the ball, the dance. They should never have danced, that was what had made them do it.

If they had never danced, they would never have kissed.

Sapphire swallowed. Not that she had any regrets, to be sure, but Maltravers certainly did. Why else had he stayed away for three whole days? Why else had he not raised the subject?

Maltravers' gaze had caught hers, and there was a knowing smile dancing on his lips. Sapphire could not help it, she smiled back, her chest warm and her body aching to be near—

"Ah, my lord, I wondered when you would get here!"

Sapphire took a step back, looking at her hand as she did so. Amethyst had stepped into the room; in all the rush of excitement of Maltravers' arrival, she had entirely forgotten that her cousin was even in the house, let alone dining with them.

Which was foolish. Amethyst had been here for years now!

"Miss de Petras," Maltravers said quietly.

"I have heard from many quarters that Lady Romeril's engagement ball was a great success," said Amethyst blithely, curtseying, then seating herself. "Do you think it was so?"

Sapphire could not help but glance at Maltravers. Was he thinking what she was? That the whole thing had been overcome, in their minds, by the kisses they had shared?

"An unparalleled success, I think," Maltravers said smoothly.

Sapphire cleared her throat as she sat, and he sat beside her. Very close. Too close.

She had never considered that there could be such a thing as too close when it came to Maltravers, but now she knew there was. His knee grazed hers, naught but his breeches and her gown to separate them.

Two layers of material. Two thin layers of fabric.

Heat rushed through Sapphire's chest and saw to her horror that her décolletage was now also starting to pink. *Why could her body not simply behave!*

"Y-Yes, I think so, too," she found herself saying, nudging Maltravers with her shoulder. "In fact, I believe it was remarkable. Very interesting indeed."

He caught her gaze and gave a smile she had never seen on his face before.

"Such a shame I was not able to see you much," said Opal, making Sapphire start. "I attempted to find you a number of times, but I suppose you were speaking with a great many people who wanted to wish you well. Did you enjoy yourselves?"

Sapphire swallowed, but before she could think what to say to such a question, Maltravers had done the unthinkable.

He had taken her stub in his hand.

"Very much so, Mrs. de Petras," said Maltravers gravely. "Any time spent with your daughter is a pleasure, but at Lady Romeril's ball, I must say I experienced…great pleasure."

Sapphire's entire body was going to explode. How could he say such a thing, and to her mother, no less!

"Mal," she breathed.

"Oh, how wonderful," said Opal, clapping her hands together and beaming. "You know, I am astonished I never saw it before! Ah, there's the gong. Shall we go in?"

Sapphire rose as rapidly as a jack in the box. That was it, a change of scenery, a chance to recollect herself. To think logically, calmly, about how she was going to approach Maltravers.

That she needed to approach Maltravers was becoming more evident with every passing moment. Though it made her cringe, she had to talk to him about…about that kiss.

Well. All of them.

The trouble was, it was impossible as the five of them sat at the table, Maltravers seated beside her. Despite their close proximity, her family did not permit private conversation.

"So tell me, my lord," said Amethyst, smiling at the earl as she sat opposite him, "how is a young lady such as myself to catch such a handsome man as yourself?"

Sapphire choked on her mouthful of roast chicken and peas.

Handsome man as yourself? What did her cousin think she was playing at?

An emotion previous unknown to Sapphire was roaring through her body, and it was only as her parents laughed and Maltravers dissembled, saying something foolish that she could not pay attention to, that Sapphire realized with a sinking feeling what it was.

Irritation. Anger. Jealousy.

Jealous of Maltravers?

This was preposterous. She wasn't jealous of Maltravers, she did not need to keep him to herself. She did not want to push Amethyst away, away from the table, out of the room…

Sapphire hesitated. Perhaps she was jealous.

"Oh, I would not call myself handsome," Maltravers was saying, discomforted, she could tell by the way he played with his food, his fork turning around and around in his hand.

When had she first noticed that about him?

"Well, I would," Sapphire found herself saying, the words tripping off her tongue so swiftly it was impossible to call them back. "I am sure I am the envy of all London."

Amethyst nodded seriously, but it was Maltravers she was interested in.

And she saw something rather remarkable. Was that another flush? Maltravers was not normally a man to get flustered, but he looked positively flustered!

"Really, Sapphy," he said, putting down his fork with a nervous laugh, as though he could no longer hold up the cutlery. "There is no need to—"

"But of course, I knew that when I eventually got married, it would be to a handsome man," Sapphire said with a teasing air, laying her stub on his arm. "And who better than the gentleman I have known for my entire life?"

Her parents laughed happily, and Amethyst mumbled something that sounded like, "Some ladies have all the luck."

But Sapphire was not interested in them. It was Maltravers she was looking at, found herself once again drawn to. Though they were seated beside each other at the table, there was still a good six inches between them. Six inches she wanted to cross.

After all, why did she have to be so far apart from him?

What was going on?

"Sapphire?" breathed Maltravers.

She nodded, unable to think about speaking. When she had first come up with the idea to falsify an engagement, Maltravers had been the first person she had thought of; the only person, in truth. Who else could she trust, that was what she had told herself. Who else would have gone along with her plan so cleverly and so carefully?

But was that all?

Sapphire stared at the gentleman who had kissed her so thoroughly just a few days ago. Had a part of her…it was scandalous to even think it, but had a part of her actually wanted to ask Maltravers, not because he would be remarkably useful for her plan, but because…she had feelings for him?

And what about him? Why was he looking at her like that, as though he would rather eat her up than the dinner before them? Why did Maltravers' gaze look through her so piercingly, as though to the very core of herself?

"Sapphire?"

If she leaned just a few more inches, she knew she could kiss him again. The table faded into the background, noise growing dull as Sapphire looked into Maltravers' dark eyes.

Eyes filled with something more interesting than a conversation about the weather, which appeared to be her parents' new topic of conversation.

Was it possible…Sapphire's breath caught in her throat as Maltravers placed his hand over her stub, holding her close. Was it possible he felt something for her?

It would make sense, she thought wildly, her ideas tangling with each other as she tried to put them all together. Why else would he have kissed her? Why else would he have agreed to go along with such a ridiculous plan?

But that also begged the question…well. If Maltravers had kissed her because he felt something akin to affection for her, then why…why had she kissed him back?

"Sapphire!"

Sapphire started, pulling away from Maltravers and looking wildly around. "What?"

Her mother was smiling as she shook her head ruefully. "I thought I would have much more time to teach you better manners before you wed, Sapphire, but we must do something about them in the time we have! I asked whether there was a story behind that beautiful engagement ring you are wearing."

"What?" repeated Sapphire blankly. "Oh."

She looked at the magnificent jewel on her hand. It sparkled in the candlelight, and she smiled. "You know, I have no idea. Perhaps Mal—Maltravers can enlighten us all."

It was a rather convenient excuse to look at him, and her stomach lurched most disconcertingly as he smiled. It was not a painful sensation. In truth, it was pleasant. Rather like how she had felt when they had been kissing in Lady Romeril's drawing room…

"It was my mother's."

Sapphire's jaw fell. "I beg your pardon?"

Maltravers nodded with a teasing smile. "I thought you would have guessed, but…yes, the ring was my mother's. Her engagement ring. From my father."

She could not believe it. This beautiful sapphire ring, once the Countess of Maltravers'—his own mother's ring? What was Mal playing at, giving her a family heirloom?

"—generous," her mother was saying with an approving nod. "And so beautiful—"

"You did not purchase it especially, then?" Jasper asked. "We did wonder, you know…sapphire for a Sapphire—"

"A happy coincidence," Maltravers said cheerfully. "And you know, when I realized what I wanted to ask Sapphire…well. I could not imagine giving you anything else."

His last words were directed at her, and Sapphire found herself smiling like an idiot.

He played the part so well.

The moment the thought rushed through her mind, Sapphire's smile disappeared and she looked at her hand and stub in her lap.

That was it, of course; she had to remember this was a pretense. A part he played, nothing more. Those kisses in Lady Romeril's drawing room were nothing more than a mistake, something they must not do again. Not that it was likely. If Maltravers had truly enjoyed kissing her, after all, would he have not visited since then?

"And now I must depart."

"What?" Sapphire said abruptly, looking up wildly as her mother shook her head at her appalling manners. "You are going?"

"Duty calls early tomorrow morning, and I must get my beauty sleep," Maltravers quipped as he rose from his seat.

Amethyst giggled, and Sapphire shot her a glare she did not entirely understand.

"I will see you to do the door," she said hurriedly, rising herself. "At least, I mean—if you are happy for me to, Mama—"

"Go on with you," said Opal.

Sapphire nodded, her heart racing as she followed Maltravers out of the dining room and down the hall where he started to pull on his greatcoat.

Why did he not say something? Anything to explain what he was thinking, what he was feeling—perhaps what she was feeling, if he could divine such a thing. If he could explain it to her, perhaps she would understand!

Maltravers opened the door. "Well, I suppose this is goodbye."

Sapphire tried to smile. "I-I'll walk you to your carriage."

There was something different between them now, Sapphire thought wretchedly as they stepped outside into the cool night air. Something had changed, their friendship altered, broken, and it could never be made whole again.

Somehow, she had ruined it. "I—"

"Yes?" Maltravers said eagerly, halting and turning to her.

Sapphire smiled weakly. "I cannot stop thinking about that kiss."

There. She had said it.

Maltravers' smile faltered, just ever so slightly. "I know. Neither can I."

Sapphire waited, but it appeared he had nothing more to say. It was infuriating! Could not the man merely explain what was rushing through his mind? Would it then become clear?

"And of course, it must not happen again," she said finally, heart sinking.

Maltravers swallowed. "No. Never."

And yet despite his words, his hands were somehow…on her waist. Sapphire blinked, trying to take in the heady sensation of his fingers, gloried in his touch, his warm, and found herself quite accidentally stepping closer to him. His chest was brushing up against hers now. Sapphire's pulse quickened, her breathing changing and she looked up in his eyes.

"Certainly not," she breathed.

"It would be a mistake, to be sure," said Maltravers, gaze flickering from eyes to lips.

She nodded, raising her hand and stub to rest on his chest, her fingers moving up to his neck, curling in his hair. "So, we are agreed, then."

He nodded, his lips lowering and getting closer, oh so achingly close to her own. "We'll never kiss again."

Sapphire almost cried out as he kissed her, slowly and reverentially this time, the same ardor yet more delicacy than before, and she clung to him, the kiss deepening, flickers of pleasure roaring through her body at the way he touched her.

He knew what she wanted. Though Sapphire hardly knew herself, had never kissed another gentleman to compare, it seemed Maltravers knew how she wanted to be kissed. His tongue teased, arched pleasure through her body and Sapphire moaned, allowing him in, welcoming the scalding heat that made her body quiver.

And then it was over. Maltravers was still looking at her, still holding her, his eyes dark in the evening shadows and something unreadable in his expression.

"It appears this is harder than we thought," he said ruefully.

Sapphire nodded, aching for him, needing more. "Perhaps we shouldn't fight it."

"Perhaps we should."

"Kiss me, damnit."

She moaned as he obeyed, as he always did. There was only one Maltravers, one man who she would permit to do this, and now she found herself craving him, craving more—

"I-I should go inside," said Sapphire, her breath ragged.

Maltravers laughed darkly, shaking his head as he reached for his carriage door. "Yes, damn it. I think that is probably a good idea."

CHAPTER TWELVE

April 15, 1816

"—AND OF COURSE, I understand why she is still living with us, I do, it's just…well, do you not think it odd? I once told Mama…"

Maltravers knew he should be paying attention.

Not just because she was his guest. That was the bare minimum of politeness, after all, giving your guest the benefit of your own attention. Particularly when they were talking.

And not only because it was Sapphire. He had never struggled to pay attention to Sapphy; if anything, he had struggled not to pay attention to her. Always conscious where she was, who she was talking to, what she was saying, whether she laughed at their jests…

But today, days after they had stood pressed up against his carriage kissing furiously as the rest of the de Petras family thought she was saying a calm farewell to him, Maltravers knew it was even more important to pay attention to Sapphire de Petras.

And not, for example, to be thinking about her lips. About kissing her. About pulling her across the dining table, lying her on it, and taking—

"Mal, are you paying attention?"

Maltravers blinked. There was a slight crease of a frown between Sapphire's eyes—eyes that were focused on him with a slight teasing look.

"Not in the slightest," he said smoothly with a lopsided grin. "You were ranting and raving about your cousin, I believe."

Sapphire rolled her eyes as she placed down her fork. "Maltravers!"

"Well, I hardly know the woman, how am I meant to keep up with all the gossip of your family?" Maltravers said, reasonably, in his mind. "Why, with each passing day there appears to be more de Petrases to keep track of!"

She giggled at that, his heart soaring in triumph at making her smile.

And managing to get through a dinner without mentioning…

"We must not speak of it," Sapphire had said firmly that night, after they had managed to finally drag themselves away from each other, and stop kissing long enough for Maltravers to step into his carriage. "No good will come of it, we just got…got…"

"Carried away?" he had supplied.

His suggestion had made her grin. "Carried away, I could not have put it better myself. We slipped into believing the ruse ourselves for a moment there, and besides, it's natural to be…"

And Maltravers had swallowed and wished he was bolder as he said, "Curious."

"Curious," said Sapphire gratefully, eagerly falling on the word as though it explained all evils in her life. "Yes, you are quite right. And now that curiosity is sated, and we have no need to ever do this—or speak of this—again."

Maltravers tried to keep his countenance calm as he smiled at Sapphire across the dining table in his London townhouse. It had been far too long, in his opinion, since she had dined with him, and though he had judiciously ensured to invite both of her parents and her cousin—Amethyst, still an unknown quantity in his mind—all three of them had, sadly, had other engagements.

The fact he had asked Edward, Coral's husband, to invite

them for dinner a day earlier, leaving out Sapphire…

Well. That was by the by.

"—not that many de Petrases," Sapphire was saying, countless silently on her fingers.

Maltravers watched closely, grasping at any opportunity—or excuse—to be looking at her. "You forgot the twins."

She blinked, a smile on her face. "How on earth did you work that out?"

"I was watching," he said quietly.

Why did that feel like such an admission of guilt? He was a clever man, he should have said. He was counting himself, something like that. Anything but admit he could not take his eyes off her, found it impossible at any given moment not to looking at Sapphire de Petras.

"Well, it was a lovely dinner," said Sapphire with a smile, pushing her plate back. "I love salmon, beautiful and light with those potatoes. And this wine, most delicious!"

"I have cake in the wings, if you wish for it."

She giggled at that. "Thank you, but I had better not eat too much—and really I should be getting home."

Maltravers' heart sank. Home? True, he had not included an evening invitation, but was it not assumed within his dinner invitation that she would spend the rest of the night here?

Not all the night, naturally. But Sapphire and himself, alone, in the dark…

Well, despite her suggestion they never veer near kissing again, they were sure to weren't they?

Maltravers' stomach lurched painfully, manhood twitching at the mere thought of Sapphire in his arms again. Still, he had not said the words on the tip of his tongue, just dancing out of reach. Still, he had not admitted what he knew he must say, eventually.

Sapphire, I love you.

But he could not say that! So bland…but he could hardly launch into a twenty-minute speech declaring his affection, could he? He had no wish to scare her off…

"You can stay here if you would like, there is no need for you to rush off," Maltravers said aloud, hating his own weakness.

If he did not say something, and soon, then he would find himself in a real bind. They had still not discussed the method of extracting themselves from this sham engagement; an engagement that became more well known, it seemed, with each passing day.

Why, after their engagement ball at Lady Romeril—an engagement ball they hardly attended, spending most of their time in the drawing room…

"Maltravers?"

Maltravers blinked. Sapphire was waving her stub before his eyes, a flicker of concern in her face.

"Just thinking," he said hastily.

"About something delightful, I'll be bound, the way you were smiling there."

Heat flushed across his cheeks. "Yes—no."

Sapphire's eyebrow arched. "Well? Which is it?"

Maltravers swallowed. "You don't have to go, you know."

That had not been what he had intended to say. He had meant to say something witty, something that would distract her from focusing too much on his expression—but instead, he had essentially asked her to stay.

Sapphire shrugged as she took another sip of wine. "I suppose my Mama will be expecting me back—"

"But you did not tell her a specific hour you would return, did you?"

She did not reply immediately. Sitting as they were opposite each other at the table, Maltravers had a clear view of Sapphire as her gaze flickered to the ring on her hand.

He could not help but look at it, too. The very physical emblem of the engagement they had entered into. At least, it would be, if the engagement was real.

There were times when he regretted giving her his mother's ring. Not that he suspected Sapphire would attempt to keep it once the ruse was ended, she was not like that. But at the same time, seeing it there, a family ring, his mother's ring, on Sapphire's finger…

Well. It almost made it feel real.

"Other people look at this ring," Sapphire said quietly, "and see a real ring. A real engagement. To them, all of this is real. No mere convenient engagement."

Maltravers' heart skipped a beat. "Y-Yes."

Why did his voice have to falter at that precise moment?

"They probably think you have invited me here, to dinner, to plan it. The wedding, I mean," said Sapphire in that same soft voice.

Maltravers swallowed. He took a large gulp of wine, perhaps too large, but he needed it. When he spoke, he wanted to ensure his voice was steady. Even if his whole body seemed to be shaking, even if he could not predict where this conversation was going.

"In fact—"

"Will you be having dessert, my lord?"

"Get out!" snapped Maltravers, quite unnecessarily, at the footman who had stepped into the dining room. "And no one is to disturb us until I call for you, is that understood?"

The footman stared, and Maltravers immediately regretted the way he had spoken. He was not a harsh master, at least, he had never considered himself so, and that was no way to speak to anyone, much less a servant.

But before he could say anything to ameliorate the situation, the footman had bowed.

"Of course, my lord," he said quietly, shutting the door behind him.

Maltravers found he was rather out of breath. His gaze shifted to Sapphire, who was a little pink. "You were saying?"

"I was?" she said blankly.

He wanted to curse to the high heavens for the opportunity he had just missed. It was outrageous, it was exhausting, it was torture being this close to Sapphire and not being in full understanding with her…

And yet he would take it, of course he would. Any chance to be close to her, even if she did not know how he adored her, made him a fortunate man.

"You were talking about planning a wedding," Maltravers gently prompted her.

He had to force himself to lean back in his chair, stop looking too eager. Because this was a conversation that could lead into very interesting direction…

Sapphire smiled. "So we would. Deciding on procession music—"

"What?"

"The music playing as I approached you down the aisle, Mal," she explained with a teasing air. "Honestly, don't you know anything about weddings?"

"Why would I?" he pointed out with a laugh. "I have not been married, and with no siblings, I have never been involved in organizing such a thing."

"Lord, I suppose you're right," Sapphire said with wide eyes. "Well, you are in luck, then, for I am a well-practiced hand. I can take care of all of it."

Maltravers swallowed. "We…we are not actually getting married, Sapphy."

Her smile fell, her cheeks pinked. "Oh. Oh, obviously."

A strange silence fell between them, and though he was desperate to break it, Maltravers was not entirely sure how.

All this talk of weddings and engagements…they had not spoken of the important things. Of love and marriage…and how they were going to untangle themselves from this fix when it no longer became possible to put off Opal de Petras into organizing the thing.

But he could not be here, in his own home, with Sapphire and no one expecting her home for several hours, without trying to take the initiative.

He had waited long enough.

"It is not the wedding, in my opinion, that is the part people should focus on anyway."

Sapphire titled her head as she examined him. "It isn't?"

Maltravers shook his head, his mouth dry. "No."

"Then you must think there's another element which is more important."

He nodded, almost smiling as he watched the curiosity spark across her face. If there was one way to guarantee catching Sapphire's attention, it was to tease her about something she did not know.

"Well?" she said impatiently with that flick of her head he knew so. "What is it?"

Maltravers took a deep breath. "Why, the marriage itself, of course."

And he watched carefully, saw a spark of understanding, saw the blush come, knew it would cover her nose first, then her cheeks, watched—or tried not to watch—as it seeped down her neck and toward her breasts.

And his heart beat faster, almost in time with her own embarrassment.

"Oh."

"Yes, if we were to marry," Maltravers said swiftly, as though it were nothing but a dull conversation between two old friends, "you would have to live here."

A smile broke out on her face as she looked around. "I can think of worse places."

"You like my home?" He had never asked, never thought to ask. It had never mattered.

It mattered now.

"I think there are few places in England better suited to a comfortable life," said Sapphire with a grin. "You always were one for luxury, Mal."

"Luxury! You cannot think me a pricked-up popinjay who—"

"You have the nicest home in London, you know that, so do

not attempt to dissemble," Sapphire said, her smile resting on his lips. Or was that just his imagination?

"Well, pleasant home or not, you would have to live with me."

"That would not be the problem."

Had he misheard? Surely, he could not have misunderstood…had she said…?

Perhaps it was time for him to be bold; take a leaf out of Sapphire's book, and say what he felt.

"Living with me would not be a problem?" he repeated quietly.

Was that a nervous laugh?

"No, that would not be the difficult thing, it would be…" Her voice trailed off, her cheeks pinking, and her gaze lowered to her lap.

Maltravers waited. Perhaps if he just remained silent, unmoving, then she would say the words on her heart, words she evidently believed he would not wish to hear. Was it possible that today, of all days, a Monday with no particular significance, would become the most important of his life?

"What?" he said, unable to wait patiently any longer. "What would prevent you from living with me, Sapphy?"

Had he sounded too desperate? Too eager?

Sapphire looked up, awkwardness in her tone he had never heard. "Well…the practicalities of marriage."

Maltravers waited, shifting in his seat, nervous energy threatening to pour from him as he attempted to be patient.

For she could not merely mean *that*, could she? There was a detail missing here, something to explain what on earth she was talking about. He watched her, Sapphire's eyes darting to the window, sunshine pouring through them, then back to him. He could almost feel the weight of her look upon his skin.

"Well," said Sapphire, her voice lowering to almost a breath. "You know."

Maltravers stared. "I do?"

For some reason, that phrase made her flush all the more, and her gaze dropped as she breathed, "Lovemaking."

Maltravers swallowed. Ah. Right. Yes. That. *Lovemaking*.

His head swam, and surely not solely due to the wine he had consumed. Lovemaking. It was not a topic they had ever discussed—as though it would even cross their minds! In truth, he could not recall ever discussing such a thing with anyone, unless you counted Micah and his many mistress, which was before Catherine's time. Well. Mostly.

But even then, he and his friend had not discussed the details.

"You do know you can talk to me about anything, Sapph." Maltravers spoke quietly, warmly, hoping with his words to encourage her to continue.

All his senses seemed pricked, eager and ready to discuss this taboo of topics with the woman he loved. After all, if not with her, then who?

There was a slight return of that boldness he knew so well in Sapphire's eyes. "I know that. It's just…well. I know that when I marry, we will—not us, I mean."

Heat flooded her cheeks, and Maltravers forced himself to stay calm. It was a slip of the tongue, that was all. No matter that it fired his heart into a roaring furnace, made anticipation tingle across his skin.

"I just…" Sapphire took a deep breath. "I do not wish to be an innocent, is what I mean. On my wedding night."

Maltravers could not help it. His jaw dropped, all expectations of what she would say utterly destroyed by the truth of what she uttered. She did not want to…

"Don't look like that!" Sapphire said with a dry laugh. "I cannot be the only lady in the *ton* who does not want to look a complete fool! As though I do not know what I am doing, and besides, I am sure it would be…you know. More enjoyable if I had even a passing idea of what I was supposed to be doing!"

Maltravers swallowed. This was not the direction he could have predicted for the conversation, but by God, he would take advantage. All it would take was a touch of honesty. Honesty that he had never managed before.

"I…I could not agree more."

Sapphire's shoulders sagged. "I knew you would understand."

"No, I mean, I *agree*." Maltravers hesitated, but forced himself to continue. If he could not be vulnerable with Sapphire as she had with him, how could he deserve her? "I mean, I do not wish to look the fool. On my wedding night."

She did not reply immediately. At least, not in words. As Maltravers watched her, half fearful she would laugh, half fearful she would rush out of the room for his ungentlemanly honesty, Sapphire did something he could not have expected.

She did rise from her chair, his chest tight as he expected her to leave, but then she stepped around the table and moved to sit beside him. Her knees brushed against his own, and Maltravers forced down the instinct to pull her onto his lap and—

"Truly?" Sapphire said quietly. "I mean…is that not unusual for a gentleman?"

Maltravers breathed a dry laugh. "Usually gentleman have had more practice."

"And you have not?"

Maltravers hesitated, his heart thumping painfully. It was tempting indeed to reveal he had been saving himself for her; that losing himself in the arms of another woman, even one who was purchased, would have felt like a betrayal.

But instead, he said softly, "I suppose I am waiting for the right person."

Sapphire nodded. "In that case, there is a perfect solution to both our problems."

Maltravers snorted. "I cannot possibly think what—"

"We share it together."

The world spun; only for a moment, but it was a heady, dizzy moment nonetheless. Maltravers found he had gripped the table as though that would prevent him from sliding off the face of the earth.

She could not have said that. It was the wine, or he was dreaming; at some point he had fallen asleep at the dining table and now he was dreaming wistfully of the words he could never hope for Sapphire to say.

"Well?"

"We share it together."

"You cannot be serious," Maltravers said weakly.

"You do not wish to?"

"That is not what I said," he said hastily. Dear God, the idea…

"Sapphire," he said quietly, taking her hand and stub in his and immediately wishing he had not, it was difficult to concentrate. "I do not think you understand what—if we—"

"I am asking you to bed me, so that I know precisely what I should be doing," said Sapphire quietly. "You would benefit also, do not forget. And I do not think you find me repugnant, we kiss well, do we not?"

Maltravers swallowed. "Y-Yes."

So well it hurt, he wanted to say. So well I want to get on my knees and beg you to—

"Then I think we can help each other," said Sapphire. "No one would need to know."

Maltravers knew it was a mistake. Lose their innocence to each other? Take the woman he loved to his bed for one night of passion, a bedding never to be repeated?

Sapphire lose her innocence? To him? It would be a mistake.

The trouble was, his whole body had been aching for her for too long. Years. And the kissing they had shared so recently—the kissing they kept telling each other they would not repeat again—certainly proved a connection he had been sure was there…

Sapphire squeezed his hand. "I am sure about this."

Maltravers took a deep breath. He was going to regret this, but his resolution was being sorely tested, and with Sapphire right there before him, asking for it…

How could he say no?

"You want me to bed you?" he asked quietly, manhood twitching at his words.

Sapphire smiled. "Bed me, Maltravers."

CHAPTER THIRTEEN

S APPHIRE STARED INTO the eyes of a man she completely
trusted. Trusted beyond what she could have expected.

Trusted to take her words and understand why she had said
them.

"You want me to bed you?"

"Bed me, Maltravers."

They still rang in her mind, shameful echoes of the words she
should have thought—or at least, should not have thought, but
most certainly should not have spoken. Was it the wine? Was that
why her head was spinning, why desire was rushing through her,
why being close to him was all she wanted?

*"I am asking you to bed me, so that I know precisely what I should
be doing. You would benefit also, do not forget. We kiss well, do we
not?"*

Maltravers was still looking at her as though she had just
confessed to murder. Perhaps he would have been less shocked if
she had done so. She had certainly crossed a line no one of the *ton*
would ever have considered appropriate.

But she wanted to know, and something about Maltravers
made it easy to ask. Easy to admit. Easy to ask him for this second
great favor which had been borne from the first.

"I want you to propose to me, Maltravers."

"Bed me, Maltravers."

Sapphire swallowed. She had said nothing but the truth when she had admitted to know what she was doing when it finally came to her wedding night. It seemed logical, at least in her mind, that one way was to be, in fact, more experienced than her future husband would expect.

He nodded.

"You…you are sure?"

The words had slipped from her mouth before she could stop them, but she had to know. This was not an agreement they could make lightly, not something they could retract once the deed was done.

Which did not explain why there was this joyful excitement, this overwhelming sense of excitement rushing through her body. Why her hand and stub felt unnaturally warm in his hands, why Maltravers' merest touch seemed to awaken something in her…

Something no man ever had before.

Maltravers nodded, not looking away. "I am."

"We never have to tell anyone, and we can keep it—"

"I am never going to tell anyone, Sapph."

Sapphire smiled. Hearing that pet name on his lips somehow made the whole thing feel far more real, far more delightful. Far more…

"Well," she said quietly. "What…what do we do now?"

For some reason, even though she had heard from his own lips that Maltravers was no more experienced than she, Sapphire looked at him with wide eyes and the expectation that he would know what to do next. After all, he was a gentleman. Even if he had not partook in lovemaking, he must surely *know*.

What else did they talk about in those clubs of theirs?

"I…we go upstairs, I suppose."

Was it her imagination, or had Maltravers' voice shook? There was certainly an odd look in his eye, something dark and delicious—

Delicious? Sapphire swallowed, tried to make her heart slow, running away with itself as it was. When had she started thinking of her closest friend as…a gentleman?

"Upstairs," said Sapphire quietly, rising to her feet. "Right—"

"Sapphire—"

"Yes?" she said quickly, looking up into Maltravers' eyes.

He had not let go of her, fingers still tight on her hand and stub. She had never permitted a gentleman to do that before.

But somehow, with Maltravers… It did not feel like a violation, it felt comforting. As though he should have been there. As though this was precisely where he ought to be.

She would go anywhere, do anything, with him.

"Sapphire, I want you to know—well, I did not expect—I mean, I did not…" Maltravers took a deep breath, and there was pain on his face as he tried to speak.

Sapphire's heart skipped a beat. *What could he need to say at this particular juncture?*

"I need you to know that I did not accept your request to help you with this, this engagement scheme so that you would…"

She watched him swallow, saw the nerves in his face, and smiled. "I know."

"Right. Good."

It appeared there was no more for him to say, and Sapphire could not think of any words either as Maltravers led her out of the dining room and into the hall. The wide, red carpeted stairs seemed to open up before her, infinitely long, leading…upstairs.

It was strange; in all her time knowing Maltravers, which to all intents and purposes was forever, she had never been upstairs at his townhouse. She had never needed to.

Now it stretched before her, a forbidden part of his world.

"Sapphire?"

Sapphire tried to smile. "Nothing, I just—"

"Come here."

She had half expected Maltravers to kiss her, and that would have been comfort enough. Having his lips on hers, an idea that would have made her laugh once, was now something she was starting, rather embarrassingly, to crave.

But he did something far more unexpected. He drew her into his arms and held her.

Sapphire breathed out slowly, the tension in her shoulders and neck melting away as she was held by Maltravers. His strength, his power, but also his gentleness. His devotion to her, as a friend. His love of her, as a friend.

Why was it so easy to lose herself in his embrace? Why was it so…so natural?

"We only have to do this if you are sure," breathed Maltravers into her ear.

Sapphire found herself smiling. All the fear, all the uncertainty had gone with the tension. She need not worry, Maltravers would be gentle with her, would never take advantage of the situation or tell anyone.

This was the gentleman in Society she was most safe with.

"I am sure," Sapphire said, pulling back but only to lift her lips to his.

Maltravers took them willingly, bestowing a reverent then not-so-reverent kiss on her. His passion, for that was the only thing it could be, even though Sapphire could not understand where it had come from, overtook her, sparking desire in her she did not understand but had no need to interrogate. It was enough that they were together, his arms around her, enclosing her in a wondrous space where only they existed.

The sound of a door closing somewhere in the house, however, swiftly brought them back to the present.

Maltravers smiled ruefully. "I suppose this is not the best place to practice."

Heat rushed through Sapphire. Maltravers, kissing her against the stairs—

"Come on."

She did not reply. She did not need to. His fingers were intertwined with hers, and he led her up the seemingly infinite staircase onto a landing lined with elegant chairs and paintings of landscapes, mountains, and lakes. A row of doors led in both directions.

Maltravers led her to the right. "Here."

Sapphire's mouth fell open. When Maltravers had suggested that they go upstairs, she had presumed it would be to a guest bedchamber, somewhere they would not be disturbed. But this was no guest bedchamber. If she was a gambling woman, she would say this was Maltravers' own bed chamber.

"Mal," she breathed, looking around the large, splendid room.

It was truly a work of art. A master painter must have spent hours here, if the ceiling was anything to go by, the spectacular cherubs and waterfall, the fruit falling from the heavens, the stars picked out at the edges as the painting seeped into a dark navy that fell down the walls.

Every part of the room appeared to have been selected for comfort, beauty, or both. There were a pair of tables on either side of the bed which had to be Chippendales and the bed itself— a four poster with a canopy of dark blue velvet. Stars had been embroidered upon it in silver thread, the evening light pouring through the large bay window making them sparkle.

Sapphire swallowed. "Beautiful."

"Yes," came Maltravers' quiet voice.

She turned to look at him, wondering what part of the room in particular he was looking at—and flushed most heartily. He was looking directly at her.

"Mal," she said quietly in a chiding tone, but it did not appear to matter.

A smile was teasing his lips. "Well. It would be churlish of me to say nothing."

Say nothing? Did that mean he had thought her beautiful before?

Sapphire said without thinking, "Now what do we do?"

She watched Maltravers hesitate, watched as uncertainty flickered across his face. Was she asking too much of him—was it possible he was doing this merely as a favor? Another favor, one in a long list of favors, now she came to think about it.

How far would her friend go to help her?

"With kissing, I suppose," Maltravers said with a lopsided smile.

Something jerked in her stomach, but it was not the painful or embarrassing lurch Sapphire had come to expect when she felt discomforted. No, this was lower and…pleasant. She could think of no better word for it.

"Well that," she jested, "we know how to do."

It did not take much for her to move into his arms; in a way, Sapphire felt she belonged there. She certainly did not like the idea of someone else moving into them, claiming the kisses she now considered her own—and in that moment, a fiery instinct of possession overtook her.

Sapphire placed her stub on his chest and wound her fingers in his hair, pulling him closer, hungrily, as she kissed him fiercely. *He was hers, and no one else's.*

For some reason, Maltravers responded in kind, hands tight on her waist, then slipping lower, lower, until they were cupping her buttocks and she gasped in his mouth, unsure how such sparks of pleasure rocked through her and knowing somehow this was different.

They had kissed before, when it had felt forbidden, dangerous, exciting—but this was new. Something she had not expected.

There was a surge of something between them now, Sapphire was vaguely aware as she lost herself in the way Maltravers' tongue teased out such exquisite and scandalous decadence from her own, and she did not know what it was.

Whatever it was, she wanted it to continue.

"Mal," she breathed as the kiss broke, immediately kissing him hard on the lips, desperate for the moment to continue.

And he moaned, and that sound did something to her, unlocked something in her she had not even realized was there, and Sapphire leaned back, pulling him with her, and Maltravers abandoned her lips but started to kiss down her neck and—

Oh, had anyone felt such sweetness, such fire? Sapphire's eyes closed, she could barely take anything else in, all she wanted was to think of him.

Maltravers. The man, her friend, kissing her so ardently it was as though he had been holding himself back all these years… Could she ever kiss another man? Would she ever be able to share herself like this, lose herself like this?

"Sapphire," Maltravers moaned as he nuzzled his lips against her collarbone.

There was a rather strange thing happening to Sapphire that she did not understand, and tried to ignore as she kissed Maltravers' neck. There was…well. A warmth, a pooling center of warmth between her legs. It was most unaccountable.

"Wh-What's next?" she managed to gasp.

Maltravers straightened up, his eyes flashing with something she did not recognize. "I-I suppose, undressing."

Sapphire swallowed. He was right, there seemed little more they could share like this—but removing her gown, before Maltravers?

She caught his gaze, and he grinned, and Sapphire immediately knew all would be well. All she had to do was trust him, and when had Maltravers ever given her cause not to trust him?

There were very few things she could not do; she had never permitted her lack of a right hand to restrict her. Except in a few things.

"I—" Sapphire swallowed, her hand reaching for the ties of her gown. She pulled, but it did not undo. There must be a knot. "Mal, I…"

Her voice trailed away, embarrassment for the first time since they had agreed to this, this…whatever it was, overcoming her. She would not ask for help. She never asked for help, not even from—

"Let me."

Sapphire blinked up into the loving face of Maltravers. Because she could not pretend not to see the affection there. He cared. She was with someone who truly cared for her.

"You have to trust me, Sapph."

Sapphire laughed. "You think I would be here if I did not?"

"I know, just…let me."

She was in half a mind to tell him the whole thing was ridiculous, that she should be gone, that she should return home. But that pool of warmth between her legs did not allow it. She had to stay, had to see where this deliciously dark path would lead her. And that meant…

Slowly, very slowly, Sapphire turned, giving Maltravers access to the ribbon holding her gown together. Her breath was tight in her chest, her hand and stub together before her, and—

"Oh…"

Sapphire could not speak, could barely breathe. As Maltravers' fingers slowly pulled the ties of her gown, his lips found a delicate part of her neck, just underneath her ear. Oh, it was heaven, to have his lips worshipping her as he slowly removed her gown.

She quivered, hardly able to believe what she was doing. And with Maltravers, of all people…

"You are so beautiful."

His words were murmured, hardly loud enough to hear, more to feel. Sapphire swallowed, heat spreading through her body as her gown slowly slipped from her shoulders and pooled to the carpet around her feet.

"Mal—

"So beautiful."

How was it possible that four simple syllables could have such an effect? Sapphire's eyelashes fluttered as she tilted her head back, willing him to kiss her neck again, aching for it.

He obliged, but he did so in a way that made Sapphire gasp. As his lips brushed once again down her neck, warm kisses leaving a trail of scalding marks, she was sure, Maltravers' fingers had moved to her chest, slowing moving her hand and stub to her sides.

And then his fingers returned to her undershift, slowly, very slowly undoing the tie at the front—and surely completely by accident, his thumb grazed one of her nipples.

"Oh!"

And pleasure, hot scalding pleasure the like she had never known before, shot through her body. Sapphire's eyes opened wide, she turned and found her mouth immediately captured, and she allowed herself to be kissed as his hands cupped her breasts, and it was all she could do not to cry out.

This was wonderful. How had she never done this before?

"Mal," Sapphire breathed, unable to think, only feel, as her undershift fell.

His fingers moved quickly now, as though he could no longer contain himself, as though reticence was no longer possible. Her stays were gone, dropped to the floor as unnecessary, and Sapphire suddenly realized she was entirely naked.

She swallowed. "Mal?"

Very slowly, she turned, a little nervous that the friend who had been by her side her entire life was about to see her, all of her, but her eyes widened as she took in the sight of…

Maltravers. James Gresley, Earl of Maltravers, a man she knew better than anyone…but apparently, not as well as she did now.

How he had managed to strip himself of all clothing while doing such hedonistic things to her, Sapphire could not tell. But he had.

There he was. All of him. Yet the expected shock—and horror—did not come. She stared at him, all of him, and it felt…right. As though their friendship had been leading to this, as though this was a natural conclusion of every day they had spent together.

"Mal," she breathed, catching his gaze.

He stepped toward her, pulling her into his arms, and Sapphire gasped at the heady tension that built in her chest at the sensation of his skin on hers. Oh, it was glorious, it was wonderful, it made every part of her want to cry out—

"I can't believe we're doing this," murmured Maltravers in between kisses.

Sapphire laughed, hardly aware of what she was saying. "Neither can I."

"Do you want to stop?"

"Don't you dare."

And somehow, they were on the bed. Sapphire could not remember how, and was certain Maltravers had not carried her, for surely she would have recalled being swept up into his arms, but here they were, the canopy of the four poster bed sparkling as a starry night, despite the warmth and light of the day, and Maltravers—

Oh, he was wonderful. Nestled as he was between her legs, her body on fire for him, on fire for his touch, Sapphire wondered how they would ever be able to resist doing this again.

Knowing now, as she did, just how he made her feel—

"Ready?"

Sapphire blinked. Maltravers was smiling, such confidence in his air, such certainty that this was right…

And it was a certainty they shared. How could she go back now, knowing what she did, feeling what she felt, embracing what they had shared—it was only right. She wanted him. This ache in her, she needed him to—

"Yes," Sapphire breathed. "Mal!"

She could not help it; though she had tried to keep her voice down from the moment they had stepped into his bedchamber, his manhood entering her was overwhelming.

Not painful. Sapphire was not sure where, but she had definitely heard that there would be pain, yet she felt none. Oh no, this was not painful.

"Sapphire?"

He had halted, paused in evident fear he had harmed her.

"Finish what you started, Mal, or I swear—"

"What?" teased Maltravers, his smile returning. "You'll stop me doing this?"

And he thrust into her and captured her nipple with his mouth, and Sapphire's back arched in uncontrolled sweet ecstasy.

"Mal!"

"Or this?"

He thrust into her again, his lips capturing hers, and she kissed him eagerly, hungrily, knowing that this warm heat of pleasure between her legs was building, and building, and she wanted him, all of him, wanted to know—

"Sapph!"

"Mal!"

Their cries intermingled as the pleasure did, and Sapphire could do nothing but hold onto the shoulders of the man she trusted beyond all others as her body rocked with pleasure, ecstasy upon ecstasy, waves of heat which shook through her, and only when it started to slow did he thrust into her, hard.

Then Maltravers fell into her arms, and Sapphire welcomed him, holding him to her chest, his head resting on her breast, and knew, with absolute finality, that she would—she could never share anything like that with any other man.

CHAPTER FOURTEEN

April 16, 1814

W HEN MALTRAVERS AWOKE, it was to find himself alone.
Alone.

It had never worried him before. Why would it? It was not as though he shared his life with another; waking up in the large four poster bed without another soul was par for the course.

But he had awoke reaching out for the warm, soft skin of Sapphire, a woman who had evidently crept out of the place when he had been sleeping.

"Finish what you started, Mal, or I swear—"

"What? You'll stop me doing this?"

Maltravers sat bolt upright. Dear God, they had—

Images flashed through his mind. Sapphire beneath him, Sapphire in his arms, her breasts in his hands, his manhood—had he really…

"Bed me, Maltravers."

A strange sort of joy, fluttering and nervous, rushed through him. Well, he had certainly not planned such a thing when he had invited Sapphire to dine, but then it had been her suggestion. Her request…

"Bed me, Maltravers."

Maltravers swallowed. If he heard of any other man who had

done such a thing, bedded a friend, a woman unmarried and unbetrothed—well, he would have called him a cad. If he had known the lady in question, he would have called the blaggard out.

Now he had done just that.

"Oh, God," he groaned, dropping his head into his hands, pressed up against his knees. "What have I done?"

It was not what he had done which was the problem, he thought bitterly. He had taken advantage of a woman he loved, a woman who had trusted him, had asked him a question he should certainly have refused, and now he had taken her innocence.

Something she could never get back.

What was Sapphire thinking this very moment? Maltravers tried to think not of the naked, squirming, moaning woman who had encircled him in this very bed, but the woman he knew her to be; proudly defiant, passionate in all she did, determined to make herself known and respected in Society.

How would she ever be respected if this was to get out?

"Because it won't, you blockhead," Maltravers told himself in a muffled voice, his lips brushing up against his hands. "She's not going to tell anyone, is she?"

And he certainly wouldn't. The last thing they needed was any of the de Petras family to find out about this—heaven forbid, Micah to hear about it. They'd be marched up the aisle within days, Maltravers knew, and Sapphire would have no choice. She would be forced to marry him, forced to follow through with the ruse they had created merely to give her a greater social standing within her family.

A slow smile crept across his face, though it was rueful.

Well, he had done it. Bedded her. Kissed her, known her far better than any other man would. *Until she married, of course.*

Forcing aside the thought of Sapphire marrying another man, Maltravers wondered whether he had…rushed things.

He had promised himself, a long time ago—before this sham engagement, before her kisses had sparked a passion he knew he could no longer ignore—that he would only ever touch Sapphire in that way once she understood precisely how he felt about her.

After he had admitted his love for her.

"I love you, Sapphire," Maltravers breathed.

Not that it mattered now. She was not here, for a start, had evidently disappeared in the early evening when they had finally exhausted themselves of all pleasure.

And it was too late now. He had wanted, craved a connection between them greater than mere physicality when they made love. Strange, now he came to think about it; apparently, he had always known they would.

But how much better to have shared such a precious moment when she knew he loved her?

Maltravers sighed. He had wanted there to be an understanding between them; in truth, he had hoped that last night would have made Sapphire admit she had feelings for him.

But she had said nothing, breathed nothing, revealed nothing.

She had clung to him, oh yes. A small smile crept across his lips as a little of his pride was restored. He certainly gave her pleasure, and it was a sweet delight to see her take it, again and again, beg for it, demand it—Sapphire certainly knew what she wanted.

So was it too late to admit his feelings? Now they were in this false engagement, one the entirety of Society believed was true, now he had quite literally taken her to his bed…

Was it too late to say something?

"Sapphire," Maltravers said sternly in the quiet and solitude of his own bedchamber.

The word echoed around the room, emphasizing terribly how alone he was.

Oh, if only she had been here when he had awoken—but he could not think of that now, he could only think of what was, not what could have been.

"Sapphire, I…" His voice trailed away as his eyes, unseeing, pictured Sapphire sitting at the end of the bed, listening to his words. "Oh, how are you supposed to tell someone you adore that you adore them?"

Why was he quick witted in all situations, save the ones that really mattered? Why was it so difficult to say what was on his heart, what he knew Sapphire would have to hear? Only then could she make a decision about this damned engagement.

Whenever in her presence, his tongue became so tied…

Maltravers smiled ruefully and forced himself from the warmth of his bed. Perhaps that was it. Perhaps the fact that he was always trying to think of what to say was the problem.

Perhaps it could be as simple as a letter…

There was a desk in one corner of his bedchamber that he rarely used. There was a study in his London townhouse, as well as one in the manor in the country, and he most often worked there if he had any paperwork that needed seeing to.

But this was no work for the estate. This was different.

A love letter.

Maltravers swallowed as he pulled on breeches and a shirt—both discarded in the heady midst of their lovemaking the previous evening—and sat at the desk. There were pens and ink there, and a raft of paper with his monogram at the top.

Well, Sapphire de Petras did something to him no other woman ever had. Surely that meant he should do something for her that he had never even considered?

Pulling a piece of paper toward him and unstopping the ink, Maltravers tried to think how one would begin such a letter.

Dear Sapphire—

He immediately crossed it out and looked at the paper again.

~~Dear Sapphire—~~

He could not be so informal, could he? No. Scrunching up the paper and throwing it to the floor, Maltravers pulled a new sheet forward.

Dear Miss de Petras—

It was immediately crossed out in turn. When was the last time he had called Sapphire "Miss de Petras?" He snorted at the very thought. Years ago, if he ever had.

No, if he was going to write a letter, a love letter, something that captured everything he adored about the woman who would still not stop dogging his every waking thought, even after bedding her…

Dear God, it only made him want her more.

Then he would have to be honest. And that meant starting in only one way.

Tongue between his teeth, brows furrowed, Maltravers lost himself in the pen and ink, all the thoughts he could never speak pouring onto the page before him.

Sapphy—

I never thought I would write anything like this, but it has become absolutely torturous for me to continue without telling you.

I should have told you years ago. When you first looked at me with that twisting smile of yours, head tilted on one side, eyes blazing—I knew then how I felt about you. We were arguing about cards and you most emphatically told me you were not cheating, which was a lie and you know it, and—

But perhaps it goes further back. When your sister was first married and you were eager to enter Society, and I realized my heart sank. Not because I would now see you more often in company, but because I would have to share you.

Sharing you never felt like an option. I wanted to keep you to myself, jealous as I was of your attention, your smiles, the way you laughed. The way you speak to the truth of every situation, Sapphy, in a way no one else I have ever met ever does.

That is the problem—you are unlike anyone else I have ever met, and I love you.

I love you.

Just three words, three words I have struggled to say but have warred within my heart for too long. You deserve to know, Sapphy, that when you asked me to propose to you I almost lost my head, heart bleeding as it was for you, and I almost revealed a secret I have kept to myself for too long.

I adore you. I need you. I want you, every day without you is barren and worthless. Arguing with you, walking with you, laughing with you, it is all that gives me life.

And now I have bedded you, just as I had always wanted to—as I dreamed of, and without even offering you my hand in truth! God, the feeling of you, the way you cried my name, it made me feel the finest gentleman in the ton. Who else has touched you, who else has managed to persuade you to remove your clothes?

And the very thought that this false engagement could be broken off—it makes me nauseous. And yet I must, I must find a way out of it, immediately. The sooner I can rid myself of this sham, the better.

This convenient engagement cannot continue.

I cannot, I will not go on without telling you how much I love you.

And I will probably never tell you. I write these words knowing in my heart that I am a coward, knowing I will never give you this letter, that the words will never be read.

But by God do I wish to.

Your ever-loving friend, who wishes he could be so much more—
J. G. Maltravers

Maltravers breathed out slowly, hardly aware that he had been holding it in.

There. It was done.

It was not pretty, nor elegant, nor refined. No poet would be impressed, no one would ever consider it elegant prose, but it was from the heart, and now he had poured out his passion onto the page, it felt wonderfully cathartic.

The desire to tell her would not disappear, of course, but it was rather a relief to get it out, somehow.

It took but a moment to fold the letter, seal it with a little wax, and after it had cooled, write her name on the outside.

Miss Sapphire de Petras.

He smiled at it wistfully. It was a letter that would never be read by anyone, but his chest felt lighter having poured it down onto paper. Knowing that in a very small way, in a way that made no sense, he had told her. He had put all his thoughts into the world.

A knock at the door made Maltravers hastily put the damned thing back on his desk before barking, "Yes?"

A footman opened the door and bowed. "A visitor for you, my lord."

Maltravers blinked. "A visitor? At this time?"

The footman cleared his throat. "It is near eleven, my lord."

Near—Maltravers glanced at the grandfather clock beside his desk and almost fell off his chair. Had he awoken late, or had he merely lost himself in the writing of his letter?

"Right, yes, fine," he said quickly, standing up and stooping to pick up his jacket. It would not matter that it was his clothes from yesterday, he had seen no one but Sapphire that day. "Where are they?"

"I placed them in the morning room, my lord."

And so it was that Maltravers hurtled downstairs, hating the thought of leaving some man waiting, and stepped into the morning room hastily without looking to see who was there before he started speaking.

"Terribly sorry to keep you…waiting."

There, standing before the window, an absolute picture of perfection with sunlight streaming around her, was Sapphire.

She turned, a wry smile on her lips, and he knew he was absolutely done for. He would have to leave London when it was all over, when the false engagement was broken. How could he bear to remain her, to see her in town every day?

"Sapphire," he breathed.

"Mal," she said with a smile. "I hope you do not—"

"I did not expect—"

"Sorry."

"No, go on," he said, chest tightening.

He had hoped this would not occur; this tension, this fraught discomfort in his stomach as they stood and looked at each other. The last time he had looked at Sapphire, she had been naked…

Maltravers forced the thought away. *That was not helping.*

"I just…hello," she said helplessly.

A smile crept across his lips. "Hello."

They had not stepped toward each other, and somehow the gap between them appeared to become a chasm; one Maltravers could not cross. Even if he wanted to. Which he didn't.

His gaze flickered to the sapphire engagement ring on her finger, and his stomach lurched. If only he had said something earlier, before kisses and lovemaking had entangled everything. Perhaps then that would be a true engagement ring on her finger…

"I just…well," said Sapphire. There was evidently something on her mind, Maltravers could see it, though precisely what he could not imagine.

Unless she regretted what had occurred between them last night so utterly that she had come to immediately break off the sham engagement. Unless it was all over.

"I don't think we should—"

"No never—"

Maltravers swallowed. So, she had no desire to repeat the experience. Well, he should not be surprised. It was outlandish, what they had done. And there was such a frown on her—

"I woke up this morning and thought there could be a child," Sapphire said in a rush.

Heat tinged Maltravers' cheeks, and he thanked God he had

thought to close the door behind him. One never knew what servants could be meandering in the hallway.

"I think that most unlikely," he said quietly, stepping toward her.

Sapphire did not precisely avoid him, but she certainly took a step back. A half step perhaps, but it was enough.

Shame flushed through Maltravers' body and his gaze dropped to the floor. *Dear God, Sapphire had never done that around him before.* Did she not trust him, did she think him unable to control himself around her?

He had managed to control himself the last few years, after all…

"You cannot know that," she said in a low voice. "We cannot know for certain—"

"I took…precautions," said Maltravers, hating how quiet his own voice had become but unable to raise it when Sapphire was so evidently nervous.

Nervous, around him. What was the world coming to?

"Precautions?"

Despite himself, he looked up and saw the curiosity he knew so well reappearing. "Yes, precautions. It…well, prevents a child. Almost all the time."

Sapphire frowned as she took a step toward him. "Now how do you know that?"

"I am a member of the Dulverton Club, and, I am sorry to say, a friend of your brother," Maltravers said dryly, trying to smile. "One picks a few things up, even if one does not intend to."

Only then did a smile crease her lips with a sigh of relief. "Good. That's good."

A prickle of pain seared his heart. Would it truly have been so awful if they had fallen with child?

The thought was madness, Maltravers told himself. Sapphire had made it perfectly clear this engagement was a means to an end, not something she herself desired. A child! A child would be most scandalous indeed, preventing her from partaking in polite

Society probably as long as she lived.

Though it was an interesting thought. A child of theirs; her boldness, her brashness, an inability to know when to stop talking…his wit, perhaps, his shyness. Her eyes. His hair.

"Maltravers?"

Maltravers coughed. "What?"

"Nothing, you just…well," said Sapphire with a short laugh. "I think I lost you there, for a moment."

"You'll never lose me."

Maltravers tried not to think about a future he could not have with her; their engagement real, a wedding swift, children. Him a part of the de Petras family, her his loving wife.

It was a dream, nothing more. One he needed to awake from.

He had not Sapphire's heart, and he would never ask her to hand it over so unwillingly.

"Well," said Sapphire, sighing heavily but smiling brightly. "No child. Well, that's a relief, is it not?"

It was on the tip of his tongue to say it was not, to cry out all the thoughts and feelings which had been trapped in his chest for too long, but Maltravers managed to stop himself just in time.

That letter upstairs, that was where his fine feelings belonged. Sapphire had asked him for a favor, to experience lovemaking, to show her, to explore together…and that is what they had done.

She was wearing his ring, his engagement ring. If she wanted the entire endeavor to be more than that, mean more than that, would she not have asked? He had never known Sapphire to hold back on what she wanted, as he had discovered in the bedsheets last night…

"Mal?"

Maltravers smiled weakly. "Yes. Yes, a great relief."

CHAPTER FIFTEEN

April 20, 1814

S APPHIRE SMILED WEAKLY. She was expected to reply, she knew, but it all felt so…so foolish. "Yes, yes, very fortunate."

"And to think I would live to see my goddaughter married," said Lady Romeril fondly.

Was it Sapphire's imagination, or did the older woman have…was that a tear in her eye? Surely not. Surely the great Lady Romeril, who was never affected by anything save bitterness, could not be crying?

"Yes, we are very pleased," said Opal with a wink to Sapphire.

She was! Lady Romeril was crying.

Sapphire's stomach churned most uncomfortably. She had not wished to attend Almack's, but her mother had insisted, and it seemed churlish to reject her suggestion when she was the only child living at home.

Well. Unless you counted Amethyst, and for some reason, Sapphire did not always count her. Which was odd, because she had attended with them, a pretty green silk gown embroidered with little daises becoming her beautifully.

She had wandered off, however, to speak to a few people Sapphire did not recognize, and that had left her with—

"Of course, when my own daughter announces her engagement, I suppose I shall have to host another engagement ball," Lady Romeril was saying.

Sapphire nodded, though her heart was not entirely in it.

For a start, it seemed increasingly unlikely Lady Rose would ever be engaged. She had shown no inclination for the married state, and had quite positively refused to attend the last three weeks at Almack's, as far as Sapphire could tell.

Why, she was worse than Emerald.

"—so pleasant to be a gentleman already known to the family," her mother was saying with a gracious smile at her daughter. "After all, we have known James since he was very small…"

Sapphire's weak smile faded. She had never pictured this, had she? In all her schemes, her plans for this ruse, her expectation she would finally be taken seriously by her family thanks to her false engagement…

She had never expected her mother to be actually *pleased*. Pleased with the engagement, yes, but she seemed absolutely delighted that it was Maltravers, of all people.

Sapphire's heart contracted painfully.

"I don't think we should—"

"No never—"

It was all a mistake, of course. She should not have been so bold, her father had always said it would be the death of her.

Well, she had been far bolder than she could ever have expected, and now she would pay the price. Now something had changed between them, if she could understand her own heart on the matter, let alone his.

"Ah, is this the young lady?"

Sapphire blinked. A woman she did not recognize had approached their small group, a curious eye roving over her.

Try as she might, just a hint of heat flushed her cheeks. Sapphire did not appreciate being gawped at by strangers, and although this woman did not permit her gaze to linger on her stub, it was still a little too close for comfort.

Still, there appeared to be no ill of her.

"Yes, this is my goddaughter, Miss de Petras," said Lady Romeril with a broad smile most unlike her. "Soon to be the Countess of Maltravers."

Sapphire smiled and curtseyed, unsure as to who this woman was. Though she was familiar; a part of the *ton,* then?

"Sapphire, may I introduce the Lady Margaret, sister of the Duke of Penshaw," said Opal quietly. "And where is His Grace? His presence is sorely missed both here and at our tables."

Sapphire's eyes widened. It was a rather presumptuous thing to say…but then, she supposed she had a sister who was a duchess and another was a marchioness. Perhaps it was not so presumptuous.

"Unfortunately, my brother has been…delayed," said Lady Margaret delicately, "in coming to town. I hear most excellent reports of your betrothed, Miss de Petras."

Sapphire tried to smile, she really did, but it was difficult, being hit with a barrage of well-wishers. Every person she had met at Almack's that evening had made a point of saying how fortunate she was to be engaged to Maltravers.

And she was.

At least, she would be, Sapphire told herself sternly, *if this engagement was real.*

If he truly wished to marry her, if the ring he had lent to her was given, rather than merely borrowed. What a world that would be…

"Th-Thank you, my lady," she forced herself to say into the awkward silence.

The woman's gaze flickered to Sapphire's stub, then back to her face, smiling gently before she curtseyed and wandered away.

"Well, to be noticed by the Lady Margaret," Opal said, squeezing her daughter's arm. "That truly is something!"

"Yes, it is I suppose a compliment to myself however, not you, Sapphire," said Lady Romeril with her more characteristic acerbic tone. "Really, the way these young misses attempt to ingratiate themselves with me…"

Sapphire stifled a smile. It was only Lady Romeril who could call a duke's sister a "young miss" without flushing.

"—Sapphire?"

She blinked. "What?"

Opal was frowning at her inattention. It appeared it would be most prescient to leave her and Lady Romeril at once. Sapphire had to get away, had to think; had to be alone with her thoughts for more than five minutes together, or she would scream.

How was she supposed to understand what on earth was going on between Maltravers and her, in her own head and heart, if she was always surrounded?

"Do excuse me," said Sapphire with a smile, "I will go and help myself to a glass of punch. May I retrieve one for you, Mama? Lady Romeril?"

Lady Romeril sniffed heartily. "Yes, I see what you are about, Miss Sapphire."

Sapphire's heart skipped a beat. *She did?* Well, perhaps Lady Romeril could advise her, for she had certainly no idea what she was about. What was she doing? What fire was she playing with, and now the match had been lit, how far would she burn?

"Y-You do?"

"I must certainly do," said Lady Romeril, drawing herself up sternly. "You wish to parade yourself around Almack's in the hope of receiving more congratulations for snaring the Maltravers boy."

Sapphire smiled weakly. Her godmother had a way with words. "You have found me out."

"I always have, I always do, and I always will," Lady Romeril said with a wink. "Go on with you."

Curtseying low to both mother and godmother—Sapphire knew how much Lady Romeril enjoyed the social niceties—she stepped away, eager to have a moment to herself.

It was not, of course, to be.

"Ah, Miss de Petras, congratulations on your—"

"—heard you managed to snag an earl! Well done you—"

"—invitations sent out yet, for we have not yet received—"

Sapphire smiled, she nodded, she murmured words of appreciation and words of agreement. She confirmed invitations had not been sent, plans had not been made, she was fortunate and he was marvelous…

Words faded into each other, faded in insignificance, and still she was not alone, still surrounded by those who wished to have an opinion, share an opinion, tell her just what her engagement meant to them, as though they were anything to do with it.

"—always knew you would make a great match," said Mrs. Loughton with a generous smile, though Sapphire noticed it did not quite reach her eyes. "I said, did I not Mrs. Howarth, how all the de Petras girls manage to make excellent matches."

"Yes, so you did," said Mrs. Howarth, her gaze raking over Sapphire in a way she did not like. She watched the older woman's gaze settle on her stub, as usual covered by a glove. "Your mother truly must tell me how she managed it, for I do not have similar luck. Unless it is something more than luck?"

Sapphire smiled sweetly at the awful woman. "I suppose my mother has the luck, Mrs. Howarth, of having pleasant daughters and pleasant manners."

She strode away before the older woman could say anything, but she heard splutters for a good minute as she continued to wend her way through the crowd.

Really, the manners of some people!

"Ah, Miss de Petras!"

Sapphire halted, sighing heavily but forcing a smile as she was once again accosted—though at least this time, the gentleman looked polite.

"A great man indeed," said a portly gentleman Sapphire could not remember the name of. "I knew his father, you know."

She smiled politely, exhaustion tugging at her eyes. How late was it? When could she realistically—and without questions— request to her mother that they return home?

"Is that so?"

"It is indeed," said the gentleman. "You barely remember him, I suppose."

Sapphire shook her head. "No, I have but vague members of the old earl."

He nodded. "Spitting image of the man, but with his mother's kindness. A rare thing."

"It is indeed," Sapphire said slowly.

"Sapphire! There you are." Amethyst rushed up to her, almost knocking the gentleman over. He strode off with a snort. "What is wrong with him? Sapphire—Sapphire, you look odd."

It was odd. How, after all these years, had she given such little thought to Maltravers' character? Why had she never noticed how *kind* he was?

Oh, she knew it, that was not the problem. If a person had asked her whether Maltravers was kind, she would have naturally said yes. No thought was necessary.

"I am very fortunate to have him as a friend," she found herself saying.

Amethyst raised an eyebrow. "My word. Do you mean the earl? I do not think I have heard of many people being friends with their future spouse. What a strange thing to say."

"Is it?" Sapphire said blankly.

Surely it should not be. Surely being friends with someone, truly friends, knowing their character and judging it as worthy of one's time and companionship, should be a prerequisite to marriage?

She should have known that—or perhaps she did, deep down, but did not know she knew it. She had certainly not thought of another person to whom she could take her idea of a sham engagement.

It had been Maltravers. Only Maltravers.

"Where is he now?"

Sapphire blinked at Amethyst's question. "The gentleman you almost knocked over?"

Her cousin snorted. "No, your betrothed! Where is the Earl

of Maltravers, I would have expected him to be at your side."

Why did her stomach twist so when Amethyst said his name? Sapphire tried to smile, tried to pretend for all the world that nothing had happened.

But it had, hadn't it? She could not pretend for long that everything was as it was; she would need to speak to Maltravers again soon, try to untangle precisely what had happened in his bedchamber…

Heat scalded her cheeks. At least, she knew what had happened. But why? After so many years of friendship, how had it been so easy for them to traverse over a line which should, in all honor, never have been crossed.

"You know, I-I do not know where he is," Sapphire said vaguely. It was an excellent question, where was he? "You know Maltravers, he not particularly interested in balls. Almack's has never appealed to him as—"

"Ah, there he is," said Amethyst with satisfaction.

Sapphire turned so violently, she cricked her neck, she was so eager to see him—yet the moment her gaze fell on him, she felt a horrible twisting pain in her heart.

Was this what heartbreak felt like? She had never expected it to be this awful, this devastating. The pain was exquisite, radiating out from her heart throughout her chest, her lungs tight, every breath agony.

There he was indeed. Maltravers, a smile on his face and laughter on his lips as…as he danced with the Lady Margaret.

Sapphire tried to calm herself, tried to remind herself that she had little cause to be so territorial over the man.

He was not her betrothed.

She may wear his ring, to the world it may appear that they had made promises to each other…but it was all naught. He owed her nothing, he had made her no promises, no commitment of any kind.

"I don't think we should—"

"No never—"

Sapphire swallowed, but the pain did not cease, only increased as she watched him stride manfully across the dancefloor at Almack's, his gaze never leaving his partner.

How did he…how could he do that?

And the overwhelming anger, anger that did not make sense yet consumed her bones, that he would even think about dancing with another, that he could touch another woman, that Lady Margaret could look at him and he at her…

Sapphire swallowed. It was impossible to conceive how she would be the same again.

But it was Maltravers. Just Maltravers.

Just the man who had always been at her side, even when her own siblings had not. Just the man who always made her laugh, calmed her when she raged, and spurred her on when she strode confidently into a room.

The man who had kissed her, loved her, showed her what it was to be held…

And only then did Sapphire know. The knowledge sliced into her heart like a knife, and yet it had always been there, had it not?

"I love him," Sapphire breathed.

Amethyst snorted, and Sapphire jumped. She had completely forgotten her cousin.

"Of course you love him," she said impatiently. "You are marrying him, aren't you?"

Sapphire stared, then turned to look back at Maltravers who was saying something in an undertone to Lady Margaret, who was smiling.

Marrying him. Marrying Maltravers.

Yes, that was what the world thought. That was what her family thought, her intention from the very beginning; to create a world in which they thought she would become the next Countess of Maltravers.

And it was foolishness, all this emotion—the false engagement had been her own idea!

"I want you to propose to me, Maltravers."

And yet, and yet…

Sapphire knew with absolute certainty, in a way she never had before, that the ruse was no longer a ruse. The sham was gone. Fallen like scales from her eyes, she now looked at Maltravers in an entirely new way.

It had started as a plan to make her parents see her as an adult, no longer the little one.

"It's quite alright, little one."

"Please do not call me that."

But it had become so much more. More than she had bargained for, though she should have known that the moment she had impulsively asked her friend of so many years to bed her.

"Finish what you started, Mal, or I swear—"

"What? You'll stop me doing this?"

She loved him. She loved Maltravers. She loved him so much it hurt to see him with another woman. To see the way she looked at him, because he was hers. Could no one see that?

Could Maltravers not see they were perfect for each other?

"Sapphire?"

Sapphire started, saw her cousin was looking at her with concern. "I am quite well."

"I'll believe that when I see it on your face," said Amethyst seriously.

A rush of affection for her cousin made Sapphire blink away most irritating tears. She had good people around her, a family that cared…but what would they do when Maltravers asked her to do what she had promised, and break off the engagement? Most inconvenient it would be, too.

Remove from her the very reason for her being, step away from the man she now knew she could not do without?

This false engagement, one she had entered into willingly, had become real.

"I truly am fine," she attempted to reassure her cousin. "It is just—seeing him, there, with…with another woman, it is—"

"I have never seen a woman so in love, you know," Amethyst

said quietly.

Sapphire smiled, blinking back the tears. She would not cry, particularly not at Almack's! "I suppose I look ridiculous right now."

"A little," said her cousin with a laugh. "But I suppose a woman so in love with a man is likely to make a fool of herself. And you have loved him for so long, this engagement is really a culmination of all that, isn't it? Of years of unspoken love."

Years?

Sapphire stared at her cousin but she could not refute her words. How could she? Amethyst had seen far more than she had.

"I think I lost you there, for a moment."

"You'll never lose me."

Oh, it would be wonderful, swanning around town with Maltravers on her arm, the man she loved always by his side, his ring on her finger…

But eventually, Sapphire realized with a sinking feeling, she would have to break it off. It would only be fair to Maltravers, she did promise. And had she not indicated he should be looking for a true partner?

"We'll need time to find real spouses! You didn't think I would prevent you from finding your own Countess, did you?"

Condemned by her own words. What was she going to do when she eventually broke off the engagement, and broke her own heart?

Chapter Sixteen

April 24, 1814

Spring was finally here. Maltravers had smelled it in the air when he had awoken that morning and it was evident as he wandered slowly down the path in Hyde Park.

Trees were budding, daffodils were pushing their heads above the earth to salute the sun, and everyone and their mother was out in their finest.

"Good day," said a gentleman as he passed, a lady on his arm.

Maltravers inclined his head but said nothing. His mind was too overcome with thoughts to consider saying a word to a perfect stranger.

After all, was that not why he had asked Sapphire to meet him here? Because finally, though it had taken him a great amount of heartache—and time—he knew there was nothing else for it.

He had to speak. He had to admit his affection.

"Sapphire, I love you."

The words would not be so difficult to say, would they? Maltravers had thought himself a man always willing and able to speak his own mind, but it appeared he was utterly mute in Sapphire's presence.

Why, he had seen her at Almack's and been unable to even

approach her!

Maltravers shook his head irritably as he wandered alone down the path. That could have been the perfect moment; they were both in public so she could not have laughed at him, at least, not any more than she might have done in private. She would have had to listen to his words, and even if she had heartily disagreed with him, she would have been able to slip off his mother's engagement ring—not Sapphire's engagement ring, no matter how much he wished it—and that could have been an end to it.

One way or the other.

The trouble was he had been unable to bring himself to do it. Almack's was too public, he had told himself at the time. What if she cried?

Maltravers' heart twisted painfully at the thought of Sapphire crying, of giving her pain.

But this had gone on long enough. He was a fool to have agreed to the false engagement in the first place…

"Please, Maltravers. I am asking you as a friend."

"Fine—fine! You had better think this through. This is a bad idea."

But he would be a far greater fool if he permitted this strange charade to continue. Not just the charade they were putting on for the world, which they appeared to be remarkably good at, now he came to think of it.

No, it was the charade in his own heart he could no longer bear.

"Good morning."

Maltravers nodded vaguely at whoever had spoken to him. He could not even have said whether it was gentleman or lady, so lost he was in his thoughts.

She had smiled at him when he had danced with Lady Margaret at Almack's, but she had been gone from the side of the ballroom when the set had finally finished. In fact, he had been unable to find her anywhere.

"Headache," her cousin had said matter-of-factly when he had inquired as to Sapphire's whereabouts. "I thought she told you?"

Maltravers' jaw tightened as he wandered down Hyde Park, no longer seeing the beauty of nature so picturesque in this morning light. How could he, when all his heart could dwell on was Sapphire?

What would she say when he finally admitted his affections? Would she laugh? Did she already know?

Was that possible? Maltravers would certainly not put it past her; was this false engagement in fact her way of sparing him the effort of having to admit his feelings?

A slow smile crept across his face. It would be the sort of thing Sapphire would do. *Oh, if only it were—*

"Maltravers, I do declare, walking about like a vagrant, up and down, up and down," came clipped tones.

Maltravers' smile broadened. There was never a bad time to see Lady Romeril, who was glaring beadily though with a hint of mischief in her eyes. No wonder she had taken Sapphire on as her goddaughter. The two were frighteningly alike.

"Lady Romeril," he said, bowing low as was due her station. And her acerbic tongue.

"Hmm," was the first reply he was given. "Not with your lady love, I see?"

"Not yet, Lady Romeril, but I intend to meet her in just a few minutes," Maltravers said smoothly.

Anything to keep the conversation light, and pleasant, and not give Lady Romeril any reason to—

"I have my eye on you, young man," said the older woman darkly. "You know Miss Sapphire is my goddaughter?"

Maltravers nodded. Half of Society was aware of that fact, partly thanks to an outburst Emerald de Petras had had, of all people. He had not been there, had heard it from Sapphire, but it appeared some rogue had been rather unfortunate in his addresses to the youngest de Petras, and Emerald had taken it upon herself to dress the fool down.

Using Lady Romeril's name as a weapon. Most unlike her.

"I would have you know, young Maltravers," continued Lady Romeril sharply, "that I would not wish the lady harmed. She is…precious to me."

Maltravers swallowed, his throat working hard to ensure his voice was clear. "As she is to me."

She nodded. "I should think so. You are engaged, after all, and you are a friend of the family and therefore a friend to me—but I warn you, Maltravers. You harm her, and you harm me. Not every engagement ends in a wedding, as I am sure you well know, and I would not have Sapphire's hopes dashed."

Dear Lord, this was intolerable! If the woman had any idea what emotions were whirling through his heart, she would surely not wish to chastise him for something he would never wish to do.

Hurt Sapphire? The thought was repugnant. It churned his stomach, making it impossible to speak.

"You are silent."

"I merely wish to collect my words before I reply, my Lady Romeril," Maltravers said, his voice hoarse. "I would never—the thought of hurting—Sapphire is safe with me, my lady. I can promise you that."

The woman narrowed her eyes. "You truly love her, then?"

And all of a sudden, it was easy. The words fell from his lips. "I love Sapphire de Petras more than anything."

Lady Romeril held his gaze for a moment, Maltravers' heart thumping wildly, and then her face broke out into a wide smile. "Damn straight, if you would pardon my French."

Maltravers' eyebrows rose. "Lady Romeril—"

"Oh, you heard nothing," she said petulantly, waving a hand. "Go on, meet with your lady love. I expect my invitation soon, and before everyone else's, you know."

Staring, attempting to speak but having no idea what words would be appropriate, Maltravers watched as Lady Romeril strode determinedly along the Hyde Park path—likely as not to accost some other young person falling under her ire.

Only then did he force himself to breathe.

Well, he had said it. Out loud, and to another person. He could never have believed it, but the love he felt for Sapphire was so strong, so great that eventually it was going to leak out of him.

And all he had to do now was tell her. A slow smile crept across Maltravers' face as joy sparked in his heart. She must feel something for him, she would never have permitted him to kiss her, to bed her if she did not.

Perhaps she just desired him. *Well*, Maltravers thought wildly, standing stock still on the path, *that was quite fine*. Desire was a perfectly sensible place to start, and she certainly liked him, they had been friends for years.

In fact—

"Maltravers!"

He knew that voice. Joy rushed through Maltravers as he turned to see Sapphire de Petras in a splendid sky-blue gown and matching pelisse and reticule. She was marching toward him as though she could not bear to be apart from for a moment longer.

Maltravers did not know what came over him. He opened up his arms, as though Sapphire was about to launch herself into his tender embrace.

This was it, the moment, and who cared whether it was in public, who cared whether all could see—let them! He was going to kiss Sapphire and—

"Ouch!"

Maltravers winced as Sapphire punched him, none too gently, on the arm. Her face was, now he came to look at it more closely, not smiling. More…furious.

What on earth was going on?

"You!"

"Me?" said Maltravers blankly. "Sapphire what—ouch!"

She had punched him again, real rage in her fist, and the ground shifted beneath him. Maltravers moved, trying to find his balance in a world that contained an angry Sapphire.

Sapphire, angry—with him?

"How dare you?" she hissed.

Maltravers blinked. *How dare he? What could he have possibly done to*—

"You cad!"

"Cad?" Maltravers repeated, reaching out to hold her as she launched herself at him.

She was out of control; he had never seen her like this, not for years, at any rate. When she had been first forbidden to attend a ball, he had sat with her that evening as she had raged at her parents' decision…but this was something more.

"Sapphire," he said urgently. "Stop!"

Sapphire stopped struggling against him, but her gaze caught his and he gasped at the intensity of her look.

It was not affectionate. Indeed, it was quite the opposite; rage burned in her bright eyes, cheeks flushed with repressed rage, from what he could see, her lips pressed together as though vicious words were attempting to pour from them.

What had happened?

Something terrible, that was clear without Sapphire needing to speak. Maltravers' mind whirled, trying to think of all the awful things that could have occurred to make Sapphire so angry, but he could think of nothing that would be connected to himself.

"Sapphire, what is wrong?" he asked urgently.

A dry, bitter laugh escaped her throat as she pulled herself from his grip, taking a step back as though she could not bear to be near him. "You have to ask that?"

Maltravers stared. Was he supposed to know? Was this something she had already told him yet forgotten—but no, he forgot nothing Sapphire told him.

"I am entirely at a loss," he said quietly, putting up his hands in surrender in case she launched herself at him again. "Sapphire, what—dear God."

The words had slipped from his mouth before he could stop them. Seemingly in reply, Sapphire had thrust her hand in her reticule and brought out a piece of paper.

At least, that was what Maltravers had thought it was to begin with. It looked like a normal piece of paper, writing on one side in black ink, an address on the reverse. Just a letter. How could a letter have caused such upset within Sapphire?

But then she waved it before his eyes, as though it were a summons of doom, and in a heart stopping moment Maltravers recognized it.

It was his letter.

Not a letter he had ever intended to post. Not a letter he had ever intended anyone to read, let alone Sapphire! His passion, his ardor, his words that poured from pen to paper in a hurried rush after he'd bedded her…

A letter he had sealed and put most firmly on his desk.

Maltravers thrust a hand through his hair wildly, trying to understand how he was seeing what was before his eyes.

When had he last seen the letter? In truth, he had not seen it in weeks. It was never going to Sapphire, so why not let it get buried with other paperwork? But she was holding it.

Maltravers swallowed. Dear God. She had read his letter. Read the words he had never planned for her to read.

I adore you. I need you. I want you, every day without you is barren and worthless. Arguing with you, walking with you, laughing with you, it is all that gives me life.

"Sapphire," he croaked.

"Do not even speak to me," Sapphire hissed, her voice low. "I cannot believe—"

"I-I can explain," Maltravers stammered.

Why did his words not come out clear? Why at this most important juncture, a moment when he absolutely had to explain himself, could his tongue not untangle itself?

Pain was radiating across his tight chest but Maltravers could do nothing to prevent it. All he could do was look at Sapphire, her cheeks reddening as she glanced at the letter in her hand before she thrust it back into her reticule.

"I cannot believe you," she said bitterly in a low voice.

"I know, I—"

"You think this jest would provoke me? You thought to tease me, to mock me?"

Maltravers stared. Mock—tease her?

Was it possible that she had completely misunderstood?

God, the feeling of you, the way you cried my name, it made me feel the finest gentleman in the ton. Who else has touched you, who else has managed to persuade you to remove your clothes?

"Sapphire, I—"

"I thought we were friends, Maltravers, best friends," said Sapphire quietly, her voice forceful as she stared at him. "I trusted you. I came to you with this engagement idea because I thought of all the people I knew, you would not make fun of me—"

"I have not—"

"And yet you write this—this diatribe of a letter which vexes me sorely!" Sapphire's eyes were wide, and to Maltravers' horror he thought he could see tears prickling at the corners. "Maltravers, how could you!"

How could he?

Maltravers was tempted to reach out again and touch Sapphire, make sure she was real. For this had to be a dream, did it not? How else would his letter suddenly appear in her hands, why else would she be looking at him like that?

As though he had betrayed her?

"How did you get that letter?" he managed to ask.

Sapphire frowned. "What does that matter?"

"Because that letter was never meant to be read!" Maltravers said, trying his best to keep his voice down, and mercifully grateful Lady Romeril had already meandered on her way through Hyde Park. "When I wrote that letter—"

"This spiteful letter, this letter designed only to mock me!"

"It is not that in the slightest!" God's teeth, but she was a difficult woman sometimes—difficult and glorious, and Maltravers could not understand where she had got it from! "I ask you again, Sapphy—"

"Do not call me that!"

"Where did you get it?"

Sapphire hesitated, just a hint of discomfort on her face. "It was delivered to me this morning in the post, of course. How else would I have it?"

Maltravers tried to think, though that was rather difficult at the moment, his heart painfully beating in his chest.

Through the post? But he had not…

Of course. The footman who had interrupted him to say that Sapphire was downstairs, he must have seen him writing it; must have assumed that he would wish it to be posted.

It was his own damned fault for writing the thing; writing it, sealing it, and writing Sapphire's name on the reverse. Maltravers almost groaned aloud with the regret of it all. How could he have been so stupid? Of course the footman thought he was doing naught but a kindness when he found the letter on his master's desk…how little he could have known what damage it would cause.

"Have you nothing to say for yourself?" Sapphire glared. "These—these words, they are ludicrous!"

Pain shot through Maltravers' heart. Ludicrous? He had poured himself into those words, bared his soul, in the knowledge—oh, the foolish knowledge—that no one else would ever see it.

But Sapphire had read it…and thought his fine feelings ludicrous.

"I do not understand," Maltravers said slowly. "Why would you read that letter and think I intended to mock you?"

There was a flash of uncertainty in her eyes. "Because…because why else would you say such things? That you intend to bed me, it was all a trick, a terrible lark to you, my scheme played right into your hands!"

"Sapphire, you do not under—"

"And I thought I was the one in control, the one with the plan!" Sapphire's eyes were wide, desperate, and Maltravers ached for her. "And all the time, you were not my friend, you merely wished to get me out of my gown—"

"That is not true!"

"The letter is in your own hand!" She glared at him, as though seeing him afresh for the first time. "Were we ever friends? Did you ever care me, at all?"

Maltravers swallowed. "More than you could ever—"

"And to think that I permitted you to—that we…betrayed, by a man I trusted!" Sapphire looked hardly able to speak. "You betrayed me, Mal, and I…I can never trust you again!"

Was it possible, though Maltravers could hardly credit it…that Sapphire did not believe the words of affection he had written in that letter? That she did not believe herself worthy of such love, such affection? That she only thought he was interested in bedding her?

"Sapphire, I—"

"It is just confusing, that is all, to read such—such things," Sapphire said wildly, cheeks reddening once more. "And after we—well, we should not have—"

"We absolutely should," said Maltravers quietly, stepping toward her.

He had to make her understand, make her see that this was all to the good. She knew now! The weight on his chest as he tried to keep his affection a secret was lifted.

They should be celebrating!

"We should not," Sapphire said firmly, her gaze dropping. "And after I-I thought I…"

Maltravers waited, heart in his mouth, but as no more words were forthcoming, he had to interject. "Yes?"

Sapphire looked away, and he saw to his horror a tear trickling down her cheek.

She was crying. He had caused such pain, such anguish, making her believe it was all some cruel jest to get inside her undergarments that she was crying—but could she not see, now, that there was nothing in his letter that would even attempt to mock her?

He could feel tension in every bone of his body, each sinew desperate to be close to her, but he had to wait. She had to understand.

"Sapphy—Sapphire, then," he corrected hastily as Sapphire turned back to shoot him a glare. "Sapphire, I…damn, woman, I wrote those words in earnest."

But she did not appear to have heard him. "And you said you must find a way out of it, immediately. "The sooner I can rid myself of this sham, the better." Maltravers, if you wanted to break off the false engagement—"

"Damn the false engagement," Maltravers growled.

What did it matter now? The false engagement, the sham, it was nothing to how they really felt about each other. And she did care for him, he was certain. Why else would she come here, meet him, rail at him for a perceived insult?

"I will not be made fun of!" Sapphire's tears were falling now, thick and fast, and Maltravers had no idea how to stop them. "You cannot understand, no one stares at you, no one gawps at you, asks you damned foolish questions—"

Maltravers' heart lurched.

"—and I trusted you, trusted you beyond anyone, and all this time—when you kissed me—Maltravers, I don't understand," said Sapphire helplessly, shrugging her shoulders as though the weight of the world rested on them. "I don't understand."

He could see that. There was confusion warring in her eyes, about the letter, about this foolish false engagement, about their kisses, the way they had lost themselves in each other…

"Sapphire, I—"

"This cannot go on," Sapphire said in almost a whisper as she stepped toward him, fire in her eyes.

And Maltravers' heart leapt as he stepped toward her in turn, certain everything had come to a head, that she would finally give into the feelings she had only just discovered—

She took his hand, and he gave it to her willingly, and such delight soared through his heart that Maltravers thought he may cry himself—

"There."

Maltravers felt a weight in his hand that was quite unlike Sapphire's hand.

The sapphire and diamond gold engagement ring was sitting heavily in his palm.

"This convenient engagement is at an end."

"Sapphire—"

"I hope that the next time you give it to someone," she said quietly, looking boldly into his astonished eyes, "you really mean it."

"Sapp—Sapphire, wait!"

Maltravers called after her, but Sapphire had picked up her skirts and ran down the path. Even if he could catch her, what could he say?

That he loved her? That the letter was a mistake, and yet not a mistake?

That she had quite broken his heart?

CHAPTER SEVENTEEN

April 29, 1814

H ER MOTHER HAD always said low moods belonged outdoors, so when Sapphire found herself sitting in the parlor, staring into space, unable to do anything save think of the words she had exchanged with Maltravers—

"—and I trusted you, trusted you beyond anyone, and all this time—when you kissed me—Maltravers, I don't understand…"

"Sapphy!"

Sapphire jumped. Her mother was standing before her, hands on hips.

"Yes?" Sapphire said a little defensively.

Opal's eyebrow raised. "Outside."

"But I—"

"Whatever mood you're in, I don't want it in here," said Opal firmly. "Come on, everyone feels better after spending a little time outdoors."

And so it was with very poor grace that Sapphire pulled on a pelisse, the warm weather still a little difficult to predict, and jammed a bonnet on her head without bothering with either hatpins or ribbon.

She was not going to ask anyone to help her. Not today.

Besides, there was only Amethyst in the house, and she was

playing the pianoforte—far better than Sapphire ever could, as had been pointed out. She smiled ruefully. Well, how would her cousin like to attempt it with one hand tied behind her back?

Sapphire breathed in deeply as she stepped outside, a gentle breeze tugging at her hair, and started to wander without much thought as to the direction of her footsteps.

"I hope that the next time you give it to someone you really mean it."

She swallowed, as though that would force the memories of her argument with Maltravers from her mind, but it was impossible.

After she had trusted him, after she had…well, loved him. First as a friend, and then something more, even if she had not known it.

How could he have teased her like that, planned such a cruel ruse—to seduce her, to take her innocence? Who else had seen that letter? A prickle of discomfort rushed up her spine which she again tried to ignore most unsuccessfully. Oh, the thought that the letter had been viewed by anyone else…

But she could not control it now. He had already teased her about affections he said he had—but how could she believe him now?

"Careful, miss!"

Sapphire halted suddenly. She had almost walked into a gentleman, paying no attention to where she was going. He adjusted his top hat which had become lopsided.

"I am sorry," she said quietly, dropping her gaze to the pavement.

The gentleman opened his mouth, evidently expecting a debate on the matter, then hesitated. "Ah. Right. Well then. Just take care, will you?"

He strode away without waiting for an answer, which was just as well for she did not intend to give him one.

Take care.

Yes, she should have taken better care of her own heart.

What had she been thinking, allowing Maltravers to kiss her like that? Touch her like that? Bed her like that…

Pushing aside the thought, and most irritating it was, that she had kissed him just as much as he had kissed her, Sapphire tried to untangle the feelings rushing through her as she continued along the pavement.

It was only recently she had even divined she had any feelings for Maltravers; but his letter. Was it true—did he speak the truth when he said he had never intended to send it to her?

"Because that letter was never meant to be read!"

But then—

"There, the cripple I told you of!"

Sapphire froze. Every bone in her body halted, feet glued to the pavement, as her head darted over to a gaggle of gentlemen who were loitering at a street corner.

One was pointing. The rest were laughing.

Heat flushed through her, undoubtedly turning her face red, and Sapphire pulled her hand and stub together, before her. They would not do anything. They would speak, yes, they would shout things probably, but they would not—

Two of the men broke off from the group and started toward her. "Hey, girly, show me your—"

"Leave me alone," Sapphire hissed, cheeks absolutely scalding.

This was ridiculous; this sort of thing did not happen on London streets!

Yet it was happening. In broad daylight, with other people passing them with heads down, evidently not wishing to get involved it what appeared to be an altercation. Sapphire could do nothing as they approached her.

Why would her feet not move? Try as she might, she could not step away, could not leave, yet she desperately wanted to, wanted to escape this quarrel—

"Come on, show me," leered one of the men, the one that pointed. "I just want to—"

"I'll pull her glove off," said the other, reaching forward.

Sapphire leaned back, desperately, half wondering whether she would simply topple backward if she could not get her feet to obey, her heart thundering so loudly she was sure passersby could hear it, and all she needed was one person to help—what had she been thinking, coming out here on her own?

And in a flash, all the precautions her family had put in place, always ensuring she never went anywhere without a chaperone, without a friend or family member, rushed into her mind, and Sapphire wished for a heart stopping moment that she was still their little one in their eyes, and that her mother not permitted her to—

"Sapphire de Petras!"

So lost in wild thoughts, Sapphire thought for a moment it was Maltravers. It would be like him, to rescue her, but as she looked around to see the speaker of her name, she was absolutely astonished to see…

Miss Antoinette Goldsmith stepped forward and slipped her arm in hers. "Did you have something to say to us, you cur?"

Her voice was sharp, aggressive, as though she regularly faced strangers in the street.

There was such force to her that the two gentlemen halted, glancing at each other as though for support. Their fellows behind them had already scarpered, disappearing into the London crowds.

"Antoinette," Sapphire breathed. "I—"

"It is as I thought, you have nothing to say to us—nothing of merit, at any rate," said Antoinette sharply to the two men. "Well, I have met with my friend now, we no longer need your assistance. Off you go."

Sapphire flicked her gaze between the sharp young woman and the two men, both of whom looked most discomforted. Without saying a word, they both turned and, grumbling in an undertone she was thankful she could not hear, disappeared in turn.

A low, slow breath. Sapphire was surprised to discover it was her own; she had evidently held her breath for far too long in the melee of panic.

"Th-Thank you," she managed to stammer.

Antoinette had already slipped her hand out of Sapphire's. "Say nothing of it," she said stiffly.

Sapphire's eyes widened. *Now, why on earth would a woman like Antoinette, no friend of hers, no friend of anyone in the de Petras family, give such a favor?*

"But you defended me," she could not help but say. "So many others passed me by and you—what made you do it?"

Her astonishment perhaps was not entirely complimentary, but she could not help it. It was not like Antoinette, as far as she knew, to do anything for another.

A slight pink creased the woman's cheeks. "I don't like you, Sapphire de Petras—"

"That much has been made obvious," said Sapphire dryly.

"—but that has nothing to do with…with your hand," continued Antoinette in a rush. She smiled awkwardly. "I would not have any woman accosted like that in the street. Even one I did not like."

Sapphire stared. It was…well, far more noble than she could have guessed, even if she had been able to make an estimation. "Well…thank you."

Antoinette frowned. "I said, say nothing of it. Good day, Miss de Petras."

"Good day, Miss—"

But she was gone, swallowed up into the London crowds.

Sapphire swallowed. Her heart was still thumping wildly, though it was starting to slow now that the immediate danger had passed.

Home. That was where she needed to go, that was where was safe.

Far swifter than she had expected, Sapphire was attempting to unbutton her pelisse and lifting her hand to remove her bonnet. It found nothing. In all the excitement, in all the panic, it had fallen from her head, dropped onto the street and she had not noticed.

"Sapphire?"

Sapphire turned and tried to smile. "Amethyst, I just—"

"Here, let me help you."

There were very few people Sapphire would permit to help her. She was no invalid, as she had told many people over the years, and did not need someone babying over her as though she could do naught for herself.

Buttons, usually, were no problem.

But in this moment, hands shaking, head ringing both with the taunts of the strangers and the harsh words she had exchanged with Maltravers—

"Hey, girly, show me your—"

"Sapphire, I—"

"This cannot go on."

Her hand shook, Sapphire unable to keep it steady, and she looked up at Amethyst with a weak smile. "Th-Thank you."

Her cousin stepped forward and silently, gently, unbuttoned the pelisse. She helped Sapphire to step out of it, placed it on the hook by the door, and smiled nervously.

"Is…is there anything else I can—"

"No," said Sapphire forcefully, then regretting her harsh tone as she saw the pain in her cousin's face, sighed. "No, thank you."

Amethyst nodded.

"You've never helped me before," Sapphire said despite herself. "Why now?"

Her cousin shrugged. "You…well, you looked upset. I did not want to ask, I know you would not wish to tell me, but I can be useful. And I…well. I am a part of this family."

A rush of sympathy roared through Sapphire. Whatever happened in life, whatever was going to happen between her and Maltravers—and she still had no idea—she would always have her family. Her parents, her siblings.

But Amethyst…she had only the charity of an aunt.

"Thank you," she said a little more softly.

Her cousin flushed. "It is your parents who have helped me understand what…well. What family is. I am glad to be a part of it."

"Amy—"

But Amethyst had slipped upstairs before Sapphire could say anymore.

She blinked up after her cousin. *Now that, she could not have predicted.*

"Coral, is that you?"

Sapphire stepped hastily toward the stairs in turn, desperate not to converse with—

"Sapphire?"

"I am just going to lie down, Mama, a headache—"

"Nonsense," said Opal decidedly, stepping into the hall. "You don't have a headache."

A flicker of irritation seared Sapphire's heart. "And how would you know that?"

Really, the cheek! To simply look at a person and state that they did not—

"Because whenever you have a headache, you keep your hand on your forehead and beg for a damp cloth dipped in lavender from Cook," said Opal with a wry smile. "Do you think I don't know you, after all these years?"

Sapphire sagged, her shoulders drooping. *Damn.* "Fine. I just want to be alone, if that is all the same to—"

"Come with me."

Her mother did not wait for an answer, it was one of her most irritating habits, but there was nothing Sapphire could do. Sighing heavily, in an attempt to show just how much she did not wish to obey, she followed Opal into the empty family parlor.

"Sit," said Opal quietly, pointing to an armchair.

Sapphire sat in very bad temper, crossing both legs and arms as she glared at her mother, who sat opposite. "Well?"

Her mother did not reply immediately, instead choosing to

delicately rearrange her skirts. Only when they were at their most delightful did she look up and smile wryly.

"This isn't like you," Opal said softly. "Staying at home all the time. I sent you out."

"You did, and then I came back."

"Why?"

Sapphire swallowed. She would not think of those brutes, of what they might have done to her if Antoinette—

The point is, they did not, she told herself firmly. It would only worry her family if she told them.

Besides, if she was forced out of doors again, the likelihood she would see Maltravers again would increase, and she had nothing to say to him. Nothing she had not said already.

"I hope that the next time you give it to someone, you really mean it."

"I was tired," she lied.

Opal frowned. "Sapphire—"

"Can a woman not decide to stay at home?" said Sapphire, throwing up her hands. "Must I have a reason to stay here, can it not simply be that I have no wish to traverse outside of this place?"

Her words echoed around the room, but they were nothing to her mother's quiet reply.

"You have never been one to hide away," she said, fixing her gaze on her daughter's. "We are not a family who runs away from things."

Sapphire swallowed, pain twisting in her heart. She was not running away from Maltravers, not really; just away from the feelings he evoked.

Which was his fault, after all! Why had he thought kissing her would be a good idea? Oh, it was wonderful when he was doing it, yes, and when they had—but she would not think of that, that was not a good idea.

It was all too confusing, too painful. She loved him? It had been a surprise to discover that, but even more of a surprise to discover that he had loved her.

Unless it was all a trick? Part of his plan to bed her?

"Sapphire," her mother said gently. "Maltravers was here."

Sapphire almost fell out of the armchair in her haste to stand, heart pumping painfully. "He was—he's still here?"

"He—"

"Tell him to go away," said Sapphire fiercely, sitting and feeling just a little ashamed at her immediate outburst.

Opal raised an eyebrow as she leaned back in her seat. "He is already gone. He said he did not wish to disturb you."

Sapphire swallowed, trying to calm her frantically beating heart, but it was impossible. Maltravers, here? What did he want? Why had he not wished to see her—had he been talking with her parents, ganging up on her, trying to convince her to…

To what? What did he want from her?

Sapphire swallowed. She knew what she wanted—at least, what she had wanted, when she had seen him dance with Lady Margaret at Almack's. She wanted him, Maltravers, all to herself. Now she did not know what she wanted.

"Sapphire, what has happened between you two?"

There was absolutely no chance, of course, that Sapphire was actually going to tell her mother anything. Tell her about the ruse, the sham engagement which had made her and the rest of the family so happy?

Tell her Maltravers had kissed her, most unaccountably—and even more unaccountably, she had kissed him back?

Tell her that in a haze of joy and conversation and wine, something had happened in her that made her want him, more than anything she had ever wanted in her life…that she had bedded him, seen him utterly naked, felt his touch, cried out in his arms—

"Nothing," Sapphire said hastily, forcing down such thoughts. "Nothing happened."

Explaining it would be impossible. She barely knew how to explain it to herself, let alone say such things to one's mother!

Though in theory, Sapphire was well aware her parents must have had to…well, do that, to have four children.

The less she thought about that, the better. She was certainly not going to say it!

"You were such good friends," said Opal quietly, persistently. Sapphire could not begrudge her the trait, it was one she had inherited. "Good friends for so long."

"Sometimes friendships end," Sapphire forced herself to say harshly.

Was it her imagination, or did her mother bite her lip?

"Good friendships can usually be mended."

"Not this time," said Sapphire darkly.

Why could her mother not leave well enough alone? Why did she have to make such a point of it? Was it not obvious that she had no wish to—

"Well, I have never seen a friendship like it, in truth," Opal said softly. "Over the years I will admit, I rather thought the connection between you would slowly fade, but if anything, it grew stronger, did it not?"

Sapphire said nothing. It was impossible to speak, impossible to explain.

Because her mother was right. It had grown stronger, and she had hardly noticed. Maltravers was just…there. Always there. A week without him was one poorly spent.

How could she been so foolish not to realize?

Opal hesitated, then said, "We—your father and I—we were delighted when we realized that you had…had fallen in love with each other."

Sapphire blinked back hot, scalding tears that threatened to fall at any moment. *Love, what did she know of it, really?*

Just the hot flustered desperate need for pleasure she had shared with Maltravers in his bed—in his own bedchamber, what had they been thinking! Just the desire, the need to be close to him. Just the agony of betrayal as she read that letter, the letter that had seemed half joke and half cruelty.

How could he have written it?

"Well," Sapphire said, almost gasping for breath as she tried to hold back her tears, "that is all very well, Mama, but you are wrong. I don't think Mal-Maltravers loves me. If he did, he would not—"

"Would not what?" said Opal sternly. "Falsify an engagement? A very convenient engagement for you, wasn't it?"

Sapphire's mouth fell open.

No. She had dreamed it; her mother did not know. No one knew, no one but her and…

"Would not offer an engagement ring," Opal continued, raising an eyebrow. "Would not continue the ruse with family, friends, even endure an engagement ball hosted by Lady Romeril?"

Sapphire had to smile. "Endure is the right word. He…he told you."

"He did," Opal said quietly. "He is in love with you, Sapphy."

Sapphire swallowed. *In love with her?* No. A gentleman, a man in love with her would not have written such things. "He is—is more of a brother, Mama—"

"Do not give me that rot," said Opal with a frown. "You have always loved him. He has always loved you. Does it really take a conversation with me to convince you of that?"

Finally, a tear managed to escape Sapphire's control, and it fell down her cheek. She loved him. Why else would it hurt so much to read such things?

I write these words knowing in my heart that I am a coward, knowing I will never give you this letter, that the words will never be read…

Oh, that he could mean such things. It was all so confusing, the lies and secrecy of their sham engagement bleeding into emotions that felt very real.

Another tear slipped down her cheek. Whatever affection was between them, it was ruined now by her misunderstanding of the letter. She should not have reacted so fiercely, Sapphire knew now, but it was too late. She had spoken, she had hurt him, and no man would ever wish to marry a woman like that.

"H-He hates me now," she choked.

"I doubt that very much," Opal said with a wry smile. "And besides, you are still engaged to him, technically you can still—Sapphire. Where is the ring? Your ring?"

Sapphire burst into tears.

Chapter Eighteen

May 2, 1814

MALTRAVERS CLEARED HIS throat and immediately changed direction, leaving the street he had just entered.

No, not today. *It was not the right weather for it*, he thought feverishly, glancing up at the sky which looked likely to rain at any moment. *No woman should have to hear such things in the rain.*

That was it. He had made his decision.

The trouble was, he had only managed to get about twenty yards down the road before he halted, groaning.

He was a coward. That was what it came down to. If he was a bolder man, a braver man, he would simply go to the de Petras house, ask to speak to Sapphire, tell her everything…

Maltravers swallowed. How could he tell her anything? After their argument in Hyde Park he had gone to see Opal de Petras and tried to make a clean breast of it. Not that the conversation had gone the way he had expected.

"You mean to tell me," Opal had said, interrupting him, "that the entire engagement is a sham? A pretense, designed by Sapphire in a foolish attempt to force herself into the realms of married women, to be taken more seriously thanks to your words James, by us? That you used your own mother's engagement ring to tie the whole thing off, and you have continued with this charade for weeks?"

And Maltravers had hesitated, and nodded. Words had not come to him.

And Opal had looked at him with that strange, unknowable look she sometimes had. She had shared a glance with her husband, and Maltravers had watched Jasper stifle a grin—a grin, when he himself was suffering from the depths of despair!

And then Opal had nodded, and said. "Good."

It had been all Maltravers could do, at the time, not to stare like an imbecile. "G-Good?"

His splutterings had been roundly ignored by Opal. "Yes, good. It's about time the two of you realized just how much you cared for each other. Now I suppose the only thing for you to do is make this sham of an engagement real…"

That had been four days ago. Maltravers had known the matriarch of the de Petras family had expected him to call again sooner; to speak, to finally make the declarations of love he should have made years ago.

And yet he had not.

How could he?

"Damn the false engagement."

"I will not be made fun of! You cannot understand, no one stares at you, no one gawps at you, asks you damned foolish questions—"

Maltravers lifted his hand and spread his palm over his waist-coat pocket. The ring in its box was still there. Of course, the likelihood that he would have dropped it was slight, but still. One could never be too careful.

He certainly had not been careful enough when it had come to looking after Sapphire. To think he had managed to get her into this damn tangle, when all she had wished to do was enjoy the benefits of a fake engagement.

Maltravers swallowed. After hiding these feelings for so long, he needed to say something. Something that was better than his damned fool of a letter…

I write these words knowing in my heart that I am a coward, know-

ing I will never give you this letter, that the words will never be read…

He groaned, startling a pair of ladies who passed him. He was a complete fool.

The misunderstanding between them, however, needed to be explained. Clearing it up between them, Maltravers knew, would not necessarily mean Sapphire would wish to marry him…there was a possibility she would never wish to see him again.

But he could not help that. She deserved to know.

Striding along the street once more to the de Petras home, Maltravers swallowed as he looked up at the front door he knew so well. Why, he had once spent an entire summer living here as a child, when his father had died. Goodness, it was strange to think that for a time, when he had not known how he would feel about her in the future, he and Sapphire had lived under one roof.

Now the same roof would be the locale in which he bared his soul, and inevitably received his marching orders.

Pain radiated through his chest. Never seeing Sapphire again. Never seeing the de Petras family again.

Somehow he had not noticed how vital they were to his happiness. He should have valued them, should have realized what he was risking when he had agreed to Sapphire's ridiculously wonderful scheme.

A slow smile crept across his face.

"Fine—fine! You had better think this through. This is a bad idea."

Almost before he realized what he was doing, Maltravers was knocking smartly on the door, his heart leaping into his mouth. Well, there was no way out of this now. Unless he simply turned and disappeared. He could leave, no one would know who had knocked—

"Ah, my lord," said Mrs. Castle the housekeeper with a smile as she opened the door. "You are expected."

Maltravers' mouth fell open. "I am—I beg your pardon?"

The housekeeper looked as confused as he felt. "You are expected. Did not the mistress write to you and ask you to visit?"

Opal, write to him? It was possible, he supposed, that she had written to him; that morning's letters were still sat on the silver tray by the door. He had completely ignored them that morning, desperate to see—

"Sapphire," he said weakly.

Sapphire froze. She was evidently leaving; there was a parasol in her hand and she was wearing her gloves. Her eyes were wide as she stared.

Maltravers knew he had to speak, but Mrs. Castle was standing right there! What was he supposed to do, with the housekeeper darting her gaze back and forth between them?

Oh, this was a nightmare!

"I think your mistress called for you, Mrs. Castle," said Maltravers weakly.

It was a pathetic lie, one Sapphire saw through immediately, if the way she rolled her eyes was any indication.

But apparently, it was convincing enough for the servant. "My mistress?"

Maltravers nodded, no longer trusting his voice. How could he, with Sapphire right there, just a few feet away?

"Miss Sapphire, could you—"

"Do not worry, Castle, I shall be sure to show his lordship the way out," said Sapphire smoothly, stepping forward to take the housekeeper's place by the door.

She fixed him with a glare. Maltravers opened his mouth, hesitated, then closed it.

Well. This was not precisely what he'd had in mind. When he had pictured the scene, for example, Sapphire had not been glaring as though she wished to burn him alive. They had been inside the house, too. They had been much closer together—

No, Maltravers thought firmly. He was not going to lose himself in dreams of Sapphire, not with the real one standing right before him.

It was time to let go of his hopes and dreams, and grasp the reality before him.

Well, not actually grasp. The last thing he needed was Sapphire shrieking the house down.

"Sapphire, I…" Maltravers wanted to groan with frustration of it all. How could he become so tongue tied around a woman he knew so well?

Perhaps if he did not care for her so much, it would be easier to spill out his heart; but then there would be nothing to spill.

Oh, damnation!

"Sapphire, who is that?"

It was her father's voice, Maltravers would have known Jasper's tones anywhere—and clearly so did his daughter.

Sapphire's face immediately went a fetching pink, darkening with each passing second, but instead of speaking to her father or telling Maltravers to leave, she did something puzzling.

"You," she snarled, grabbing Maltravers' collar with her hand. "Come with me."

Maltravers had no opportunity to speak, heart thumping wildly as Sapphire half pulled, half dragged him around the side of the house.

He had just decided to attempt to say something, anything, when Sapphire pushed open a gate and pulled him through it, releasing him only to close the gate behind her.

Maltravers looked around. They were standing in the de Petras garden. He had not been out here this year, the weather had been far too inclement, but he recognized the rose bushes, the climbing wisteria up the back of the house, the bench where he and Sapphire had spent so many happy summers.

Summers that, it appeared, were never to be repeated…

"What?"

Maltravers turned to see Sapphire glaring, her arms crossed as she narrowed her eyes.

Well. This was it. He was unlikely, after all, to have a better opportunity to speak to the woman he loved, even if the heavens looked like they were about to open at any moment.

And he would always regret it, always, if he stayed silent.

"I-I am sorry," Maltravers said quietly. "About the letter."

If possible, Sapphire flushed an even darker red. Oh, his thoughtless pen. If only he had considered, even for a moment, the impact on the woman he loved if she had the misfortune to read his ill-considered words.

"Your teasing letter does not concern—" Sapphire began stiffly.

But he could not permit her to continue. "I was not teasing, Sapphire, I—damn."

Maltravers could not help but swear as he ran a hand through his hair. This was not supposed to be so difficult!

There she stood, Sapphire, in a pretty blue gown that made her eyes shimmer. Perfectly accentuating the waist that, but for a few weeks ago, he had his hands on. Oh, to touch her again, to feel her warmth beneath his—

Get a grip, man! Maltravers thought darkly. If he was not able to pull his mind from the gutter, then he was going to lose all opportunity he was now giving himself to try to explain!

"Sapphire," he said heavily.

Sapphire raised an eyebrow. "My Lord Maltravers," she said mockingly.

"I love you."

She stared, eyes widening, and Maltravers knew she had guessed but not been sure.

Hope rose, fingers tingling with anticipation. Finally, he would make his case.

"I have been in love with you for as long as I can remember," Maltravers said quietly.

He stepped closer, unable to help himself, but Sapphire mirrored him, stepping back.

He must not rush this.

"Being in love with you, Sapphy, is glorious and painful," he continued with a wry laugh, his eyes raking over her face as he attempted to guess her feelings as he poured out his heart. "Glorious because everything about you is—well, it's perfect. You are so beautiful, so clever, so wonderful—no one has ever made me laugh like you."

Was that a flicker of a smile?

It was gone before Maltravers could look at it properly, but he was certain that just for a moment, Sapphire had smiled. Emboldened, he took another step closer to her. This time, she did not back away.

"Painful," Maltravers continued quietly, not taking his eyes from her, "because being so close to you and knowing you did not feel the same, knowing you saw me as a brother—"

"I did," Sapphire breathed.

And it broke his heart to hear it, though Maltravers had known it, but he could not stop now. All he had to do was finish this ridiculous speech, know Sapphire heard it, and leave. Leave London, perhaps. There was nothing else for him here but her.

"Painful because the older we grew, the more I knew I would never be happy unless I could be by your side for the rest of your life," said Maltravers with a bleak smile. "Lord, when you came to me with your idea about a sham engagement—"

"I should never have asked you to—"

"I am glad you did," Maltravers forcefully. *Could she not see?* "Glad, Sapphire, don't you understand? Oh, it was perfect, the perfect opportunity for me to be close to you, to—it was all I wanted!"

Sapphire's mouth fell open. Her cheeks were still colored, pink rather than red, and Maltravers hoped beyond anything she could see the truth in his eyes, hear it in his voice.

"It was so perfect that I did not stop to think," Maltravers admitted, a dry laugh escaping his lips as his fingers reached to pull her into his arms. "I didn't think about the consequences, about what could occur if I did not control myself, and when I kissed you—"

"I kissed you back," Sapphire breathed.

Maltravers' heart soared. "I could not believe it, I thought I was taking advantage of you, but I could not stop myself, I craved you—"

How could he say these things to her? And yet, how could he not; didn't Sapphire deserve to that he was utterly in her spell?

"—and when we made love—"

"That," Sapphire interrupted sharply, "was never part of the plan. Never part of my plan, I mean, the engagement, and—oh, Maltravers, I should never have asked you—"

"I told you before, I am glad you did," Maltravers said softly.

She looked up, eyes wide, trusting.

"It was perfect," Maltravers breathed. "You are perfect."

"Not so perfect. My temper—"

"Is what makes you who you are," he said quietly. "Sapphire, you do know that the thought of you marrying someone else, anyone else, is painful?"

Sapphire swallowed. "No."

"Well, now you do," he said, unable to help himself, he lifted a hand to cup her chin. "I…damnit, I cannot say it any other way."

"Then don't," she breathed, not pulling away from his touch.

Maltravers' heart skipped a beat. "I want you to marry me."

"I am," Sapphire said, a teasing smile on her lips.

He groaned. *The woman could be so infuriating!* "No, I do not mean—hang the sham engagement, I already told your mother—"

"I know," she said darkly, "and you are going to pay for that, I hope you realize."

Pay for that? Oh, Maltravers must absolutely not think about the myriad of ways she could make him—

"I said that I want to marry you," he said again.

"And I said that I am."

How did she do this? Torture him with sweetness yet sensual delight in her eyes?

"No," Maltravers said quietly, "I mean, for real. No sham engagement."

He waited, heart in his mouth, hardly able to breathe. *There. He had said it.* And when she told him, kindly he was sure, there was no possibility of her ever thinking of him in that—

"I know," Sapphire said, lifting her hand to his face, stroking his cheek. It was all he could do to stay still and not immediately crush her lips with his. "I want to marry you, Mal."

Maltravers blinked. "I beg your pardon?"

And she laughed, and he could feel her laughing, and that made no sense for how could he—and then he realized he had pulled Sapphire into his arms without thought, for was that not where she belonged?

"James Gresley, Earl of Maltravers, I could not imagine loving anyone else," Sapphire said. "Marry me, Mal. Marry me for real. Marry me so that I can spend the rest of my days annoying you—"

"Kissing me," he said, his chest tightening at the thought. "And more—"

"Oh, and more," she breathed, lifting up her lips.

He needed no further invitation. Almost moaning at the desperate need which had been held back for so long, Maltravers kissed Sapphire hard on the mouth, his hands already dropped to her buttocks to cup her toward his manhood, and his whole body cried out in pleasure, in agony, to know that this was the beginning of the rest of his life.

With Sapphire in his arms.

How long they stood there, he did not know. What did time matter to them?

Eventually, however, Sapphire broke the kiss and beamed. "I think I am going to need that ring back."

He could not get it out of his pocket quick enough; it had lain there the moment she had handed it back to him, and Maltravers' heart soared as he pushed his mother's engagement ring back onto Sapphire's finger.

"Does this mean I need to start learning to call you James?"

"I think I would find it strange to have you call me anything but Maltravers."

And as he pulled her close once more, his questing lips desperate to find sweet relief in the delicate pleasure of her mouth, sunshine burst through the clouds.

It was not going to rain after all.

CHAPTER NINETEEN

May 18, 1814

S APPHIRE SIGHED HAPPILY. "You…you do not think they'll be too upset, do you?"

"What business is it of theirs if they are?" Maltravers shrugged, his movement shifting Sapphire ever so slightly as she leaned against his shoulder. "We are happy. That is the important thing."

Happy.

Sapphire could not have imagined such happiness. In all her years, after knowing the man for so long and never realizing the unsettled feeling in her stomach that she always felt when looking at him was something far more than genteel pleasure at his company, how could she be happier?

"Happy," Sapphire said quietly, taking Maltravers' hand and squeezing it. "Yes, we are happy."

The carriage rattled, the road less cared for this far from London, but she paid little heed to it. There was little that could distract her now. All her senses were heightened whenever she was with Maltravers; how could she have gone so long without noticing?

At least, without realizing quite what it meant.

Sapphire smiled, her fingers intertwined with his, unable to stop herself but finally realizing that there was no need to. Now that all the misunderstandings were uncovered, now they knew, both of them, how desperately they needed the other. Now they were about to—

"Oh dear."

Sapphire looked up into the teasing eyes of the man she loved. "What?"

"You're smiling," said Maltravers evenly. "That means you're plotting something."

She could not help but laugh at his ridiculous suggestion. "Maltravers! You know I am only smiling because I am here with you, you dolt!"

"And that," he said, leaning for a kiss, "is precisely what I wanted to hear…"

Time was a difficult thing to keep track of in a carriage. The fields passed by, different with each passing hour, but Sapphire spent very little time looking out the window.

When she had such a delightfully handsome and charming man beside her—one who knew precisely how to kiss, how his fingers could tease her and tempt her, why bother looking at the countryside?

"I still cannot believe it sometimes," she breathed.

"What?"

"You."

In truth, she also could not believe they had made the decision they had. It was only a few days ago that they had come down on it, a decision they knew would have ramifications across the entirety of her family, but it felt…

Right.

Now they were here, committed, she would not have it any other way.

"You did not mention this to anyone, did you?"

"Mmm?"

Sapphire smiled. Maltravers was being slowly lulled to sleep by the gentle rocking of the carriage. Or perhaps, more likely, it was because she had kept him awake half the night at that inn, demanding more and more pleasure…

"I said, did you mention this to anyone?" she said, nudging him with a laugh. "Mal!"

"Is this what married life is going to be like with you?" he jested. "Constant nagging?"

She nudged him again, harder, and giggled as he let out a mock groan. "Yes, if you don't answer my questions! I would have no need to nag if you simply—"

"I did not tell a soul," said Maltravers with a laugh. "And you?"

Sapphire shook her head, a smile dancing on her lips.

It had felt rather rebellious, not telling anyone. A part of her had wished to include Amethyst on the secret—she was part of the family, after all, and felt more a part of it with each passing day.

But she had not been entirely sure her cousin would have kept it to herself, and the last thing they wanted was to be discovered before they had managed to get there.

"Oh, no, I tell a lie. I told someone."

Sapphire stiffened. That was the trouble with Maltravers, he always surprised her, even if she did not wish him to!

"Who?" she asked urgently.

A slow smile crept across Maltravers' lips, and Sapphire wondered how she had ever not known how desperately she loved him. *Delightful, infuriating man!*

"Amber."

Sapphire laughed, despite herself. "Amber? Mal, she is only a few years old!"

Maltravers nodded sagely. "I thought she had a right to know, as the heir to the de Petras line—"

"Oh, Coral will love you for that—"

"Besides," he said with a laugh. "I did not think it likely that she would tell anyone."

She kissed him hard on the mouth to stop his nonsense, and

quivered as pleasure started to tingle through her body.

It was possible, she knew, for lovers to tire of each other. It happened, though rarely, even in love matches, though her parents were an excellent example of how affection could be maintained over years—even with children.

But passion did not always remain. Micah was a prime example of that; the man had moved through several mistresses, from what Sapphire had been able to tell from the whispered gossip she had overheard, before he had found Catherine.

But surely no such thing could occur with her and Maltravers. Why, it was like they were made for each other! In a way, perhaps they had been.

Perhaps over the years they had been smoothed by each other's edges, like two stones in a river, becoming closer and closer over time.

Sapphire moaned as his hand moved up her thigh. "Mal, we mustn't!"

"Who says?" he growled under his breath.

It was several minutes before Sapphire was able to think or speak, after he so carefully brought her to ecstasy with his fingers, and she grinned lazily at him, body heavy with desire.

"You'll have to be careful," she teased. "You'll wear me out."

The carriage rocked again as Maltravers laughed. "I think that most unlikely."

The faintest of kisses was brushed against her lips, and Sapphire sighed. Had she ever been this content? It was difficult to imagine a world in which she was more joyful, more at peace, more wildly content.

Marrying her best friend, the man who had seen her at her best—and worse. Her future husband.

The very near future.

"I cannot believe it."

Maltravers glanced at her, his hand still resting on her thigh. "What do you mean?"

"Well, this," said Sapphire, gesturing around the rocking

carriage. "You, me, that we could be so perfect for each other."

He raised an eyebrow and laughed. "I knew," he pointed out.

Sapphire punched him ever so gently on the arm. *Well, he deserved it.* "So why did you not say anything sooner?"

"Because," said Maltravers in a tone that suggested he was going to make a clear and well-reasoned argument, "I am an idiot."

Sapphire giggled as he joined with her laughter, joy soaring through every inch of her.

He truly was—but then, she had been, too. It seemed ridiculous now she looked back that she had not noticed it; not noticed his affection, the love that had stirred in her heart. So many months, perhaps years that they could have been this happy.

Well, they would simply have to make the most of it now.

"Sapphy, I think—" Maltravers leaned forwards, blocking the view from the window as he examined it. "Yes. I think we're here."

Sapphire's stomach lurched. She had known they would arrive eventually, of course, but had not expected it to be so soon.

How long had they been on the road, two days? Three? It was hard to keep track, with such a delightful companion.

"We're here," repeated Maltravers softly as he leaned back and smiled.

Sapphire nodded, not trusting her own voice to speak. *They were here.* After the wild idea that had struck her, after convincing Maltravers—not that it had taken much—after frantically packing, leaving her parents' home, no longer her home, at the crack of dawn, after days on the road…

They were here.

To think it had all led to this. Every conversation, every laugh, every moment she had looked at him and felt glorious, as though nothing could exceed these sensations…

Every kiss. Each had led her to here.

The carriage slowly rumbled to a stop, Sapphire's heart beating so loudly she was certain Maltravers would hear it. He opened the carriage door and stepped outside.

The scent of freshly cut lawn, and ash, and iron, rushed into the carriage, only succeeding in increasing Sapphire's heartbeat. They were here, it was not a dream…

"Sapphy?"

A hand appeared in the carriage door. Maltravers' hand.

Carefully, trying her best not to step on her skirts and trip into his arms—not that it would be a hardship—Sapphire took Maltravers' hand and stepped out of the carriage.

A pretty little village met her eyes as she acclimatized to the bright sunlight.

Just a village. She had not been entirely sure what she had expected, but it was not this. A place so normal. One could not have picked it out as a special place. But it was.

"Sapphy?"

There was just a hint of nerves in Maltravers' voice, and for some strange reason, it made Sapphire smile.

He could always be honest with her, and she with him. They would not have to hide their feelings for each other anymore; they could return to that state of openness they had enjoyed as friends, but with even more possibilities.

More pleasure.

"Maltravers," she said, smiling up into his dark eyes.

His fingers tightened around hers. "So, are you ready for Gretna Green, Miss de Petras?"

Sapphire beamed. "Not Miss de Petras for very long."

"You are certain?" Maltravers' eyes looked worried, even as he pulled her into his arms. "You will take my name? It is a great break from your family's tradition."

She nodded. "I want to build new traditions, new ways of doing things. With you."

And before he could say anything, Sapphire kissed Maltravers hard on the mouth. Their last kiss before they became man and wife.

They kissed probably for far too long—at least, when they

finally broke apart, Sapphire noticed to her horror, that they had attracted a few curious glances.

"Well then," said Maltravers a little hoarsely. "Time to make this convenient engagement into a marriage."

And they walked, hand in hand, toward the blacksmiths.

EPILOGUE

August 24, 1814

O*PAL…*

"—cannot believe you did it!" Opal said, eyes wide as she embraced her baby daughter. "Eloped—and took Maltravers' name, Sapphire how could you?"

She was no longer her baby. Really, it had been several years since Sapphire qualified for that term, but surely every mother had the same challenge. Once a child, always a child in a mother's heart.

Sapphire Gresley, Countess of Maltravers, however, certainly no longer looked like the "little one" her family had always called her.

Dressed in the most elegant of gowns with a silk choker at her throat and that huge sapphire engagement ring on her hand, Sapphire beamed at her family as she hugged as many of them as she could manage.

"Oh, Mama, I am sorry that—Coral!—we eloped, but you must understand—"

"And now there are no more daughters to give away," quipped Jasper.

Opal shot a glare at her husband, but it softened as she saw his teasing air.

He was right. As Emerald stepped forward for her embrace with the youngest de Petras—*at least of that generation, there were now five grandchildren,* Opal thought fondly—she had to admit that in a way, it was an end of an era.

All her children married.

And to good people. Opal's eyes roved over the group which had collected in their parlor, the first day after Sapphire and James had returned from Scotland.

There was Robert, Emerald's husband, tall and usually serious but laughing as he slapped James on the back. "I am astonished you thought our approach so worthy as to copy us!"

"Copy you? You must be joking, it was more a desire to escape the long months of wedding planning," James laughed, shaking back his head, his dark hair slightly too long after his month sojourn in Scotland.

There was Edward, Coral's husband, holding one of Micah's twins as her mother stood nearby with a nervous expression.

Opal smiled. Catherine was a wonderful daughter-in-law, she truly could not have hoped for better. Pretty, elegant, refined, and far more sensible than half her children put together. And twins! That girl would have her hands full and no mistake.

"Did you hear that, Sapphy?"

Opal watched as her youngest daughter looked up from a conversation she was having with her niece, Amber.

"This blaggard—"

"Maltravers!"

"—is saying we copied him in eloping! Him and Emerald!"

Sapphire smiled wickedly. "And so what if we did? A marvelous idea it was, too, escaping from Mama's plotting—"

"Sapphy!" Opal frowned at her wayward daughter, but shrugged with a laugh as James stepped across the room and kissed his wife full on the mouth.

Well, one could not argue with true love. *Even if Sapphire had attempted to do so,* Opal though ruefully. She would not be the first in this family, now she came to think of it.

Why, she had been forced to speak sense to each of her four children over the years. Without her interference—and it was hardly interference, more a good natured push in the right direction…

Well. Perhaps none of them would have married.

"No, in truth, I merely wished for a little time on my own," Sapphire was saying to Coral with a laugh. "Without the entirety of the *ton* watching! You know, Lady Romeril threatened to come to Scotland and make us do our vows again!"

"A wise idea," said Opal dryly. "I would probably have come with her if she had been so bold, I rather think I missed out!"

It was difficult to keep at bay the slight hint of bitterness in her voice.

She was not an overbearing mother…at least, she did not believe herself to be. But it was hard not to notice that of her four children, only two of them had been married from this house. With her in attendance.

Sapphire's smile softened, and she slipped from her husband's embrace to cross the room, smiling wistfully at her mother. "You are not truly angry?"

Opal looked into the brilliant eyes of her daughter, and wondered whether she would ever be able to be truly angry at any of her children. They were so dear to her; each of them a walking, talking amalgamation of herself and the man she loved so completely.

She caught Jasper's eye over Sapphire's shoulder and stifled a grin. There was something about having your heart walking about in pieces around the world. No matter what they did, as long as they came home, all would be well.

"I am not angry," said Opal gently. "Would I have preferred to be there, yes—"

"Mama, you are angry!"

"But you had to make the decision on your own," she continued with mock severity. "Something you are rather good at, if you ask me!"

Sapphire giggled, and Opal's heart twisted. *Oh, her daughters—her son. Their daughters!*

The de Petras family, growing and expanding and still just as much full of love as it had been when she and Jasper had first wed. How was it possible for one's heart to continue expanding, with each new member of the family?

"Congratulations," came a quiet voice.

Opal looked around to see that her niece had approached, a little nervous it appeared.

Sapphire beamed. "Amethyst, thank you!"

"Time on your own, y'say?" muttered Micah from the other side of the room, loud enough for them all to hear. "And how well are you managing that, exactly?"

A chuckle radiated through the room.

Opal laughed herself. Well, he was right. She could not deny it. How many of them were there now—fifteen? And if she was not very much mistaken, Coral would soon have another familial announcement in that department…

Sapphire and Amethyst were chattering away, about what Opal could not quite hear, and she stepped away quietly to allow them a little privacy. These young folks, as she had told Lady Romeril only the only day, did not wish for all their conversations to be continuously overheard. They needed privacy, or at least the feeling of it.

Instead, she approached the man who looked happiest in the room. "Well done, James."

James Gresley, Earl of Maltravers beamed, eyes bright. "Well, we got there in the end, I suppose."

"And a long time coming it certainly was," said Opal seriously.

Truly, she had never seen two people who loved each other more make such a hash of discovering their mutual affection. It had been agony watching them step around it like fools, but there it was. There was no accounting for sense when it came to this sort of thing.

"You're part of the family now, you know. Officially."

James' chest puffed out. "I know, Mrs. de Petras."

Opal tapped the young man on the shoulder. "Come on, James, I have known you since you were born, and you are now one of my sons-in-law. The least you could do is call me Opal!"

One never quite knew, did one, who one's children would fall in love with?

There were no guarantees when it came to love, let alone the love of another. She was relieved, now they were all wed, to see that they were all pleasant people!

But though she would never admit it—certainly not to her children—James would probably become her favorite. After seeing him so young, holding him as a newborn in her arms, watching him grow, seeing him overcome the pain of his parents' loss, then falling in love with her own daughter…

"I am not sure I will ever get accustomed to that," admitted James ruefully. "I shall have to think of a pet name for you."

Opal narrowed her eyes. "Don't you dare."

"How about Mother de Petras?" shot Edward from across the room, a mischievous look on his face.

She pointed a finger at the naughty young man. "Don't you dare, Edward!"

"Or Mama Petras," teased Robert, stepping carefully out of harm's way, though it was Jasper in the end who punched him good naturedly. "Ouch!"

"No less than you deserve," murmured Emerald.

Opal laughed. That was her Emerald; shy she may be, but when it came to speaking, she always had the right words to say.

"Don't you start ganging up on the men in this family, Papa, there aren't enough of us to go around," quipped Micah, sitting in an armchair, his other twin in his arms.

"There certainly is not," said James ruefully. "Though I believe…well. We may have an answer for that."

Opal's heart skipped a beat as Sapphire stepped toward her husband and took his hand, a most uncharacteristically shy expression on her face.

No. Surely not; they would not announce it this early, they would not even know this recently from the wedding, would they? Unless…ah…

"We are having a baby," said Sapphire with a nervous grin.

"Oh, Sapphy!"

Almost as one, the entirely family stepped forward and laughed as they fought to embrace the youngest de Petras sibling as mingled cries of celebration poured out.

"Another baby!"

"Congratulations—"

"—not surprised in the slightest—"

"When, do you have any idea when?"

"More de Petras cousins!"

Opal could not help but giggle as she watched the medley of nonsense before her. After all their misunderstandings, after Coral and Micah's inability to talk to each other without sniping, after Emerald's shyness threatened to separate her from the family, after Amethyst's sudden arrival…

Everything seemed to be falling into place.

A chaotic place, of course, though that was only to be expected. Opal watched with a joyful heart as Amber and Beryl chased each other around an armchair, giggling wildly as they never quite managed to catch each other.

The twins would be growing soon, and with Sapphire's little one on the way…

"I think it's time to make an announcement," Opal said quietly.

All the excitement seemed to melt away. Silence fell in the parlor.

Opal swallowed. She had not intended to make her statement sound quite so dramatic, but every eye was now upon her—some looking far more worried than others.

"Opal," Jasper said quietly.

She knew precisely what he was going to say; that they had

agreed today was not the time. But when would there be a better? They were all here, weren't they, and it was getting harder and harder to collect all her children together.

They needed to hear this. They needed to know.

"Mama?" said Coral uncertainly.

Opal smiled. "Please do not concern yourself, it is nothing serious—at least, it is serious, but—"

"Serious?" repeated Emerald, and Opal saw the color drain from her daughter's cheeks. "How serious—you are not ill, Mama?"

"I am not ill," she reassured her. "It is only—"

"Because you have mentioned how cold you felt yesterday and it was a warm day," said Amethyst, with almost just as much concern.

Opal smiled. She did not need any further proof that she and Jasper had made the right decision, they knew in their hearts that they should have done it a year ago or more…

"I promise you I am well, Amethyst," she said gently. "But it is you that this affects."

Her niece's eyes widened, her cheeks pinking as the eyes of the rest of the family turned to her.

Opal hesitated. She knew how difficult it had been for her children to acclimatize to having Amethyst here, but they had embraced her warmly—even Micah, over time.

And now she was about to change it all.

"What is it, Mama?" asked her son quietly.

Opal smiled and reached out a hand. Just as she had known he would, Jasper took it immediately. "We are moving."

"Moving?" repeated Sapphire with wide eyes.

"Moving?" said Amethyst, her mouth falling open. "Moving to where?"

Jasper squeezed Opal's hand, and she stole a glance at him before she continued. He was her strength, her comfort in all times. Even when they had misunderstood each other, when it had seemed as though they would never be able to find each other again…he was always there.

"In truth, we tire of London," Opal admitted with a dry laugh. "We have lived in the city too long, tiring of these endless balls, dinners, card parties, picnics, walks, rides—"

"Always at Lady Romeril's beck and call whenever she wishes," said Jasper.

Opal shot him a look, though it softened as the rest of the family laughed. "Quite. Well, we have bought a house—"

"A palace," said her husband wryly.

"Fie, Jasper, you know it is no such thing!" she said with a laugh. "A large manor is probably the only way I would—"

"Huge."

"Large enough for you all to visit," she continued, shaking her head with a smile. "And Amethyst, you are very welcome to come with us. Very welcome. You are still a part of this family."

For some strange reason, her breath caught in her throat, her lungs tight. Her gaze was fixed on Amethyst; the niece with no parents, who had nowhere to go when they had taken her in.

Would she consider this a rejection, too?

Amethyst wallowed. "I…I am grateful for the offer, Aunt. Leaving London would indeed be a shame, but—"

"Then don't."

Opal turned to look at Coral, trying to keep her surprise hidden. *What on earth was Coral talking about?*

Her eldest daughter had that determined look on her face that always meant she was going to get her own way.

"Don't?" said Amethyst.

Coral nodded. "Stay with us. We have more than enough room, you can stay at Glaenarm House even when we are in the country, if you wish to."

"No, stay with us," said Micah. "John is boarding now, his bedchamber is—"

"We have room, we'd love to have Amethyst," said Sapphire impetuously. "Would we not, Mal?"

"Wouldn't dare argue otherwise," said James cheerfully.

"After all, family—"

"But if Amethyst wants a little peace and quiet, she should stay with us," interrupted Emerald in her quiet but strong-minded voice. "Stay with us, Amy."

A lump rose in Opal's throat as she watched her four children bicker happily about who would get to take in their cousin, Amethyst's red cheeks paired with a smile of wonder.

Her children. They were not perfect, no; she would never claim that. At least, most of the time. Sometimes Lady Romeril did become quite provoking.

But they were hers, and they understood as she did the power and importance of family. They would not leave their cousin to be dragged to what was clearly in their eyes dullness and boredom.

"I will have to change around each home every week," Amethyst was saying with a laugh. "Then it will be fair!"

"That's not the worst idea," grinned Edward.

His wife turned on him. "Edward Barlow, do not be ridiculous! We cannot have Amethyst traipsing about London—"

"We all have carriages," pointed out Robert.

"Lord, yes, so we do," said Sapphire with a laugh. "Well then, how about it?"

Amethyst looked between them, tears sparkling in her eyes. "Y-You would all do that for me?"

Opal swallowed. *She was not going to cry.* It was not in her nature, though she was certainly overcome.

Coral stepped forward and took Amethyst's hand, squeezing it. "We are the de Petrases."

"Most of us," said Sapphire with a grin.

Coral glared. "Our lives may end up being a bit of a saga—"

"Never a truer word spoken," muttered Catherine darkly.

"—but we stand by each other!" Coral said amongst the laughter. "You should know this by now, Amy."

Amethyst nodded and Opal sighed happily as she stepped away from the young ones and sat on the sofa, her husband joining her.

"I do not think we could have planned that better ourselves," Jasper murmured.

Opal rested her head on his shoulder. "No. No, I don't think we could."

From this place of warmth and love, she looked at the brood of de Petrases, still laughing and arguing about who was going to host Amethyst—it really did look as though they would take in turns—and Opal knew she could not be happier.

This was what she had wanted. A home, a family, the opportunity to make right the mistakes her parents had made. No pitting siblings against each other, never that.

Building them up, together. Seeing them succeed, together.

"Well, it is settled then!" Amethyst's cheeks were pink, but she looked mightily pleased. "As long—well, if you do not mind, Aunt Opal?"

Opal waved a hand. "Whatever makes you happy, my dear."

"I suppose you will rather enjoy having a little time to yourselves," said her niece with a shy smile. "After all, it must be years since it was just the two of you. Tell me, I have never heard the tale. How did you meet?"

Jasper chuckled as Micah groaned. "Oh, Lord, we could be here for hours!"

"That is indeed a mistake," said Sapphire confidently as she moved to sit opposite her parents.

"Even I know it by heart," James said with a laugh.

"Not that I have told it that often, so you must have heard it from my mischievous daughter," said Opal with a grin as the rest of the family settled in seats around the parlor.

The parlor where Sapphire had learned to walk, where Micah and Coral had bickered, where Emerald had lost herself over and over again in her books. Where their grandchildren played.

Opal took a deep breath. "Besides, it is not that story that is the most interesting."

Amethyst leaned forward. "It isn't?"

Jasper took her hand in his and squeezed it. Opal squeezed it back. *How fortunate she was.*

"I would say the most interesting story is from after we met," said Opal with a smile. "After Jasper had been declared legally dead—that's the one you want to know…"

Start the de Petras Saga all over again—or for the first time—by returning to Opal and Jasper's story in THE MISPLACED HUSBAND.

About Emily E K Murdoch

If you love falling in love, then you've come to the right place.

I am a historian and writer and have a varied career to date: from examining medieval manuscripts to designing museum exhibitions, to working as a researcher for the BBC to working for the National Trust.

My books range from England 1050 to Texas 1848, and I can't wait for you to fall in love with my heroes and heroines!

Follow me on twitter and instagram @emilyekmurdoch, find me on facebook at facebook.com/theemilyekmurdoch, and read my blog at www.emilyekmurdoch.com.